EXPO '98

Sherlock Holmes in Omaha

A Novel

by

Berkley Forsythe

Berkley Forsythe

Simmons-Boardman Books, Inc.
1809 Capitol Avenue, Omaha, Nebraska 68102

First Edition, First Printing September 1987
ISBN 0-911382-05-4
Library of Congress Catalog Card Number: 87-090737

©1987 Berkley Forsythe. All rights reserved. No part of this book may be reproduced or transmitted in any form or by any means, electronic or mechanical, including photocopying, recording, or by an information storage or retrieval system without written permission from the author.

DEDICATION

Just as Dr. Watson was dedicated in the daily writing of his letters to his beloved wife, Mary, so this book is dedicated to my own wife, Mary — who is not nearly so patient as the doctor's wife, but who is equally kind and loving.

ACKNOWLEDGEMENTS

Dr. Watson was wounded during the battle at Maiward in Afghanistan. He was felled by a bullet from a jezail rifle. Had he not been wounded, he would not have been discharged from Her Majesty's armed forces, and hence would never have met Sherlock Holmes — forever depriving the world of the Master's adventures.

To commemorate this most fortuitous event, the Nebraska Scion chapter of the Baker Street Irregulars combined the two words to form their official name — the Maiward Jezails.

I accordingly give sincere thanks to Richard D. Lesh, Commandant of the Nebraska chapter of the Baker Street Irregulars (The Maiwand Jezails Scion Society), and members Richard Nastase, Merrill Edgerly and George Lynch for their comments and suggestions on reviewing "Expo '98".

The author is especially indebted to the Western Heritage Museum, which is housed in the same Union Station that President McKinley arrived at in October of 1898. Its permanent display of the great Trans-Mississippi and International Exposition of 1898 was a true inspiration. Also, special thanks to Debbie O'Donnell, who made available actual copies of the Omaha Bee News daily newspapers published during that important year. Dates and events cited in this work were quoted as Dr. Watson would have read them from these editions.

And of course I am deeply indebted to the late John H. Watson, M.D., for the detailed journals that he so thoughtfully left behind, as well as the late A. Conan Doyle, M.D., for the inspiration that he created for all of us to enjoy for all time.

FOREWORD

During the summer of 1983, a burned-out old two-story home north of the downtown district of Omaha, Nebraska, was ordered to be destroyed as unfit for human habitation. As the bulldozer was knocking down the last vestige of a foundation, a metal box popped from the wall where it had been secreted some eighty-five years earlier. The property owner was a friend of mine, who knew of my interest in Omaha history, as well as in writing. I have prepared this text from these materials hopefully in the same manner, if not precisely the same style, as Dr. Watson himself might have done.

I traced the ownership of the home back to its original inhabitants, a couple named John and Clara Thoms. When John dropped dead suddenly in 1894,

Clara converted it to a rooming house, to support her and her three small daughters.

I located Clara's sole surviving offspring, a lady of 90, in an Omaha area nursing home. I am honoring her family's request to protect her anonymity. But she told me that she had a clear recollection as a very small child of her mother renting rooms during the Spring of 1898 to an English doctor named Watson. However, the excitement of the great Trans-Mississippi Exposition was her chief memory of that year.

She also recalled that the doctor had only one patient — a strange man in his mid-thirties named Sherlock Holmes. He always wore disguises when he left the boarding house, but preferred tweeds and a strange hat when he stayed home.

"After President McKinley left town," the lady recalled, "Dr. Watson, Mr. Holmes and mama took a metal box to the basement. Then the two men went away." She paused for a moment, and looked as if some faint and distant memory was trying to emerge from her failing brain. "Oh, yes," she finally said. "Mr. Holmes promised to come back from England and marry mama."

This possibility ended when Clara Thoms died as the twentieth century was being born. The house was sold, and her three small children were raised by an aunt. The home went through a series of ownership changes and, ironically, was last used once again as a rooming house. A fire of mysterious origin during the winter of 1982-1983 ended its current history, but fortunately unlocked its colorful past.

The following was a letter which I found on top of Dr. Watson's copious journals:
"October 15, 1898:
To whosoever finds this metal box:

If President McKinley — God bless that fool-hardy man — should still be in office when you discover this, you must read no further, but rather re-seal the box and secrete it somewhere, telling no one. It is of the utmost national security — I dare-say, it is for the safety of many nations —that these documents be suppressed for many years, if not indeed for all time.

I shudder as I realize the risks that I am taking in preserving these manuscripts. But I am too much the historian not to record such data, especially since I seem to be the only person at a most remark-able moment of history interested in preserving the data on such a monumental case.

However, should sufficient time have passed that the nation will not be in jeopardy from these revelations, then sir (or madam, whichever the case may be), you have my full permission in advance to do what you will with these memoirs. Publish them as they are, if that is your wont. Or put them in some narrative form, which of course was the vehi-cle I have personally always preferred.

Since I was not present during some of these strange goings-on, I necessarily had on occasion to rely on second-hand accounts from others. How-ever, I pride myself on being an excellent judge of character, and I assure you that I have used infor-mation only from people of impeccable character, so I can vouch that their information is as truthful as that to which I can personally attest.

The fate of the nation may be in your hands, just as it is now in mine. I must close now. Sherlock Holmes and the interminable widow Thoms inform me that the tomb is now ready for my precious metal box.

I remain, John H. Watson, M.D."

CHAPTER ONE

It was a particularly disagreeable day in April in the year 1898. A sharp wind blew a slow but steady rain till the sheets of water were at times horizontal, seeming to defy the laws of gravity. To complicate the situation, my beloved wife Mary, who is always an open and agreeable soul, was obviously acting secretive and somewhat distressed about a matter which she could not quite bring herself to articulate. I was finally on the verge of saying, "For Queen Victoria's sake, woman, spit it out," when a familiar heavy knocking occurred at the front door.

"Don't knock it down, Holmes," I shouted, as I clambered to my feet as fast as my invalid leg would permit. I don't know why I bothered, because as usual my dear Mary was already showing our dripping friend the hospitality of our living room.

"A man could drown out there, my good fellow, before that game leg of yours came around," Holmes shouted in unbridled good humour. He collapsed his bumbershoot, and slipped out of his coat, both of which Mary promptly tended to.

"I'm surprised you'd leave 221b on a day like this," I said with amazement, "let alone travel all the way to our humble quarters."

"I've got some good news for you," Holmes said, producing a rather lengthy telegram from a dry pocket. "You are going to America."

"What?" I cried with disbelief. "Now, why in the world would I want to go to America?"

"Because you are being honored at the largest convention of your compatriots — "

"Great heavens," I interrupted with amazement.

"— at the largest World's Fair ever."

"I don't appreciate this sort of twitting," I retorted gruffly.

"Surely you don't think I would jest about a matter of this gravity," Holmes said with what appeared to be bruised feelings. "My good doctor, won't you at least read the wire?"

Still thinking this to be some sort of sadistic trick on Holmes' part, I unfolded the document and read aloud.

"The Honorable Sherlock Holmes, 221b Baker Street, London, England: Our kindest regards. We are interested in soliciting the services of your friend and biographer, the honorable John H. Watson, M.D. It is our desire to have him act as both Commissioner and Guest Speaker at what promises to be the largest convention of his fellow homeopaths ever to assemble. Ours will hopefully be the largest of nearly one hundred conventions to meet at Omaha, Nebraska, U.S.A., in conjunction with the great Trans-Mississippi and International Exposition to be held June 1 through November 1 of this year. Since we do not possess Dr. Watson's address, we hope that you will serve as our intermediary to expedite this matter. We wish to maintain an element of surprise and expectation for our members, so it will be most appreciated if Dr. Watson would travel under the assumed name of Charles Mitchell, Veterinarian, and proceed first to Minneapolis, Minnesota, where our committee will explain his duties to him. All travel and lodging arrangements have been made in advance for himself and a companion in anticipation of his affirmative answer to this singular honor. Of course, Dr. Watson will be paid a handsome stipend for his services. Hopefully yours, Clinton C. Farnham M.D., Chairman for Pre-planning, Homeopath Convention, 1898."

"What an extraordinary honor," Mary said with unfeigned admiration. "Of course you will accept. And perhaps Mr. Holmes would be kind enough to accompany you."

"I'm afraid that's quite out of the question," Holmes replied. "You see, I received a second telegram today as well. It seems that the Paris police are in need of my consulting services for most of the summer. We will be travelling in quite opposite directions, my friend."

"Pity," I replied. "However, I don't intend to accept in any case."

"Nonsense," Holmes replied emphatically. "This sort of honor is bestowed perhaps once in a century. Your stature as a man of medicine will be forever engraved in history."

I must confess that my ego swelled out of all proportion as the magnitude of the honor settled into my consciousness. "I suppose you're right, as usual," I said, my chest expanding to the point of endangering the buttons on my shirt. "Oh, very well," I said with some feigned modesty. "My sweet Mary and I shall make a second honeymoon of it."

"I'm afraid," Mary said, slipping back into her earlier evasive manner, "that is equally out of the question. I've been trying, somewhat unsuccessfully I fear, to explain to you a project I have agreed to undertake."

"What," I demanded in a somewhat conceited tone, "could possibly be more important than seeing your husband accept the greatest of laurels from his colleagues?"

"Mrs. Cecil Forrester, my former employer, has taken quite ill, I've been informed," Mary explained. "I've agreed to care for her during what promises to be an extended convalescence." Mary dropped her eyes shyly, and continued, "So, you see, I would not be spending much time with you this summer in any case."

She could not have deflated my puffed-up arrogance more neatly with a hatpin. Here I was, all concerned with my own self-importance, and my sweet Mary was pledged to do her Christian duty to her former benefactress. Was ever a non-deserving man such as I blessed with an angel like Mary?

Next day the weather cleared somewhat, and I wired my hearty acceptance to Dr. Farnham in Omaha, Nebraska, U.S.A. However, as the time grew closer to my sailing date, I must confess that both Mary and I had misgivings on more than one occasion. The conflict between Spain and America had been worsening by the day. The American battleship "Maine" had been blown up in Havana harbor on April 11th. America had blockaded the harbor, and shots were routinely being exchanged. On April 26th, three days before my departure date, America formally declared war. Parliament waffled on whether to ally itself with its English speaking former colony, or with its European neighbor. Both Mary and I feared that should England flop to the side of Spain, I could well find myself fifteen hundred miles behind enemy lines. Then there was the risk of naval war. Either Spanish or American warships could attack my liner on the basis of English neutrality, if for no better reason.

We convinced ourselves that the naval threat was negligible, since the daily papers reported the fleets of both nations were concentrated in the southern latitudes, hundreds of miles from the London-to-New York sea lanes.

As to the unity with Spain, that seemed to be less likely with each passing day. In its typical active neutrality, the Mother Country was on the one hand promising the colonists non-intervention, and at the same time supplying the Spanish fleet, for profit of course, with collier ships laden with coal. Both countries seemed to be satisfied, if not elated, with the arrangement.

In any case, when my liner prepared to sail for New York, one Charles Mitchell, Veterinarian, was listed among the passengers.

CHAPTER TWO

Sherlock Holmes and Mary saw me off at the pier. Holmes was armed with both my ticket for the States and his own for the continent, which would leave shortly before mine. Mary was to be taken to her former mistress' home by a trusted cabby, once Holmes and I had separately departed.

As I gazed at my new identity, I mused, "This appears to be more of a mystery perhaps than the one you are embarking on, Holmes."

"All life is a mystery of sorts," Holmes observed. "Pity more of the mystery isn't a greater challenge."

"Still it seems strange that I'm off to what will undoubtedly prove to be a mundane World's Fair," I said, "while you are off to mad adventure in Paris, without, I might add, the benefit of my usual chronicaling."

"I promise to keep excellent notes for a change," Holmes replied. "I don't approve of your hopeless romanticizing of my cases, but I confess that you are the only person who has accurately reported my deductive approach to criminal investigation."

"I only report the facts," I said with indignation.

"As you see them, I'm afraid," Holmes smiled. "In any case, be assured that you will be supplied with the facts as they occur. I'm certain that the gendarmes of Paris will be as eager to take credit for my future work as Scotland Yard has in the past."

"You are too easy on the devils, if you ask me," I ventured.

"As long as I have you, my dear friend, my ego shall never suffer," Holmes replied. "I must leave you and Mary to your farewells. My ship sails immediately. Have a good trip."

Holmes vanished into the crowd that always accompanies departures of large liners. Mary and I bid our sad good-byes. And I embarked on what would prove to be the greatest adventure of my life.

At first I thought that I should perish before the ship half reached New York — if not from the sea-sickness that cleared my system the first two days, then from the boredom of the next two. Also, the ship employees who attended my every need would surely smother me with their constant attention, as it seems my American employers would have me travel in no way but first class. How I could endure ten days of such torture was beyond my understanding.

However, on the fifth day, a friendly but aging couple introduced me to shuffleboard by day and whist by night, both of which proved to be as addictive as Holmes' cursed cocaine. And by the seventh day, I was so accustomed to being molly-coddled by my ship attendants, that I would be mildly irritated if someone failed to shuffle my whist cards for me.

In fact, the last half of the trip would have been completely delightful had it not been for a most disagreeable old man. True, he was horribly de-formed, which would affect the humour of even the most pleasantly dispositioned person. But he was so alternately angry and then anti-social, that I could not help wonder why he bothered to take a voyage at all. Indeed, I had seen saner people than he on my infrequent tours of Bedlam. Fortunately, most of the time he merely sat in a deck chair and glared at the other passengers. Even more fortunately, he would hibernate in his room for hours at a time, thereby providing blessed relief for us all.

From the time we docked on the pier at New York, until I was duly ensconced in an equally ele-gant compartment on a train for Minneapolis, my every need was seen to on the same grand scale as I had experienced on the liner. As I slipped into slumber, with the train wheels beating a lullably on the tracks, I dreamed that I was indeed royalty.

My mood could not have been more buoyant when I emerged from my compartment to enjoy a delightful breakfast. Unfortunately, as I looked up from my first bite of American bacon and eggs —a dish of which I am still hopelessly fond — my eyes met those of the disagreeable old invalid from the ship. I determined that I would not let him spoil my breakfast, let alone the entire trip to Minneapolis. How would my dear Mary look on this, I mused? For one, she would certainly pray for the poor fellow. Then, too, only charitable and hopeful thoughts would enter her mind. Perhaps he was traveling to some clinic, where a master surgeon would restore his twisted body. Perhaps, then, he would be so rejuvenated as to live a life of singular importance, perchance to lead the world one day to permanent peace.

Such mental gymnastics restored my appetite as well as my feeling of royalty, and my mood was once again as glorious as before. The pathetic old fellow no longer affected me unfavorably, but in fact gave me a strange feeling of elation.

About halfway to Chicago, however, I began to detect another antagonism which could not be so easily dispelled. I began to get the feeling that I was being watched by someone — someone certainly other than the cantankerous old man. Reasoning as I thought that Holmes might, I took to meandering off the train at each stop. I would stretch, buy some tobacco, visit with a stranger, then re-board the train at the last possible moment. After performing this ritual two or three times, I finally isolated my man, who at each stop would surreptiously board the train a few cars away as soon as I had done the same.

He was really not the sort one would expect in this line of work. He was portly, red-faced, and dirty — very much like a miner from Newcastle. I rather thought that Holmes would be proud of me for having ascertained not only that I was being fol-lowed, but perceiving such an unlikely fellow to be my pursuer. Chicago was the next stop, and I determined to shake this would-be nemesis from my trail.

I studied the timetables for departures from Chicago, and detected that a train bound for Omaha, Nebraska, would be rendevousing shortly with my train to Minneapolis. If I could somehow convince my grubby friend that I was going to change trains, I could perhaps have him detour himself to Omaha whilst I continued on my way to Minneapolis as planned.

As I had done the previous several stops, I once again departed the train, this time working my way toward the ticket office. When I was certain that my pursuer was well within hearing, I enquired of the price of a ticket to Omaha.

As I purchased my fare, the loudspeaker blared, "Mr. Sam Lynch, please call your client, Mr. Nastase. I repeat. Mr. Sam Lynch, it is urgent that you call your client, Mr. Nastase."

Having completed my transaction, I glanced casually around to see if my fellow traveler was still with me. Perceiving that he was temporarily neglecting his duties, I plunged into the crowd toward my train to Minneapolis, convinced that this fellow would board the train to Omaha, and cease to be a bother to me.

Suddenly a hand from the crowd clutched my shoulder in a vise-grip that could not be denied. I turned to stare into the piercing eyes of the ill-tempered twisted man.

"See here," I exclaimed. "I have been as patient as can be expected of any man. If you must resort to being physically abusive, I shall have to summon the police."

"Quick, Watson," a familiar voice shot out from this pathetic creature. "We haven't a moment to lose."

I found myself being propelled into a secluded corner, as the man who had to be Sherlock Holmes signalled to some accomplice. For a moment, I thought that I might be looking into a mirror, as a man who could have been my twin brother, dressed almost identically to me down to my vest, stepped past us. When my double was certain that my shadow had seen him, he casually returned to the train that was bound for Minneapolis and boarded it. My pursuer glanced around, then climbed on the train a few cars away at the last possible moment.

"You are getting to be too clever, Watson," the old man said, his limbs suddenly as miraculously healed as I had previously imagined. "You almost diverted our dirty friend to the proper track. Come, my friend, or we will miss our train to Omaha."

CHAPTER THREE

When we were once again housed in yet another luxurious private train compartment, I demanded more information from my old friend.

"Sorry to be so devious, Watson," Holmes apologized, as he removed his wig and make-up. "But I assure you that it was of the utmost necessity."

"Surely you could have let me in on your little charade," I said, more than a bit miffed. "You've treated me rather like a small child."

"And you have played your part to perfection, my friend," Holmes replied, "as I knew you would. No, Watson. I could not risk your reacting even a blink to my disguise. And my travelling incognito I assure you was of extreme importance."

"How so?" I demanded to know. My question was punctuated by a rapping on our compartment door.

"Aha," Holmes said, rushing to greet our visitor. A huge man of portly build filled our doorway. "Captain Lewellen, I presume?"

"At your service, Mr. Holmes," the Captain saluted.

"Please come in," Holmes beckoned. "May I present Dr. John H. Watson, also formerly of the military service." Out of sheer habit I returned his salute. "Captain Lewellen will be in charge of security at the Trans-Mississippi Exposition."

"I see," I acknowledged.

"And a most difficult job that promises to be," the Captain added. "Thank the gods that you and Dr. Watson were available to be of service to us."

"Our pleasure," Holmes replied. "European crime has appeared to hit an all-time low. Right, Watson?"

"I can't say that a return to law and order distresses me all that much," I replied. "But tell me, Holmes. Why your disguises? And who was the filthy fellow who was following me?"

"Ah, yes," Holmes said, wiping the last of the grease paint from his face. "It was my suggestion that you be invited to the Exposition under a pseudonym. You see, from what Captain Lewellen informed me, I was reasonably certain that our enemy would intercept the telegram he sent to me."

"A lot of good it did you," I chortled. "They obviously saw through my alias almost instantly."

"I was counting on it," Holmes replied, "just so they didn't penetrate mine. By the by, I thought that I was a perfectly marvelous crotchety old man. Didn't you?"

"You very nearly ruined my trip," I acknowledged.

"Actually, remaining under cover permitted me to see who would be watching you," Holmes continued. "On the boat, you were left quite alone. At first I suspected the elderly couple who took you in, but it was obvious that they simply took pity on your pathetic loneliness."

"I beg your pardon," I bristled. "I'll have you know that I was quite content."

"But the grubby chap on the train was another story," Holmes went on. "I had him pegged from the outset. While he was busy following you, I searched his compartment, and found his name to be Sam Lynch."

"That's the fellow who was paged in the Chicago terminal," I noted.

"Quite astute, Watson," Holmes congratulated me. "And I was the person who had him paged."

"That's odd," I mused. "I could have sworn that the page was from his client, a Mr. Nastase, as I recall."

"Once again, my idea," Holmes chuckled. "A certain Mr. Nastase is an attorney in New York who represents the mainland interests for many powerful Cubans who have profited heavily from cooperating with the Spaniards occupying their island."

"Then you knew that this fellow Lynch was working for him?" I asked somewhat amazed.

"I know it now," Holmes said. "Actually, I was virtually certain from the beginning. He boarded the train in New York. He had a distinct accent characteristic of a place called the Bronx. And his calendar had a notation on today's date that simply said 'lawyer'. Since I had to extract you from his pursuit in any case, I thought it prudent to confirm my suspicions at the same time. I had Lewellen employ your look-alike and arrange to have them waiting for us at the terminal in Chicago. By the time Mr. Lynch unmasks the fake Dr. Watson, he will be hopelessly on his way to Minneapolis."

"But surely he knows we went to Omaha," I said. "It will be a simple matter for him to purchase a ticket in Minneapolis, and once again be in pursuit."

"No," Holmes wagged his head. "We have seen the last of the filthy Mr. Lynch. Now that we have penetrated his disguise, he is of no use to his client. But now we can be quite confident that the Cuban nationals will have other representatives in Omaha for our amusement this summer."

"That is really quite marvelous," I applauded him.

"Quite elementary, actually, my dear Watson. Now, Captain Lewellen. How are things progressing in Omaha?"

"Not very well, I'm afraid," Lewellen replied with a frown. "We have one thing in our favor, however. Thanks to the war, the President will not be at the grand opening of the Exposition."

"The President?" I asked, somewhat astonished. "You can't mean President McKinley, surely?"

"The same," Captain Lewellen sighed.

"And our client, I might add," Holmes said. "Although he is not totally aware of it."

"But he is almost certain to visit the Exposition some time this summer, war or no," the Captain went on. "So we have our work cut out for us in any event."

"I apologize for interrupting," I said, "but did you say that President McKinley is our client, Holmes?"

"Quite so," Holmes replied. "I was approached on his behalf by the American embassy in London. It appears that his life will be heavily at risk when he visits the Exposition in Omaha this summer. I determined that I would be of most use working undercover in any case. So I concocted this story of you addressing the homeopath convention, which will indeed be meeting in June."

"Then — you mean — ," I stammered. "Then I am not to be honored?" My ego was utterly shattered.

"Actually, you are to be honored," Captain Lewellen interrupted. "I mentioned it to the powers that be, and you have been asked to address the opening session of the convention — that is, if you agree to accept."

"Well," I choked once or twice. "Of course, I would be singularly honored. Please inform them that I accept."

"Now," said Holmes, "pray bring us up-to-date on the events in Omaha, Captain Lewellen."

"Well," the Captain cleared his throat, "the latest I'm afraid to say is murder."

"Murder?" I echoed.

"Actually, double murder," the Captain replied. "Of the most hideous kind." Holmes' face lit up as if he had just received the best sort of news —which of course he had, for the fellow fairly thrived on mysterious murders.

One must forgive Holmes if it appears that he delights in the butchering of these poor devils. In his defense, one must remember that his finely honed mind thirsts to be used, and that the prospect of it being challenged produces a kind of euphoria in the man that could be easily mistaken for glee over someone else's truly dreadful misfortune.

"Pray go on," Holmes gently prodded him.

"For some time now, we've had a series of bizarre animal killings," the Captain said, puffing steadily at his pipe. "Always near the Exposition site, where of course construction is continuing twenty-four hours a day. First a chicken, then a lamb — followed by a goat and a sheep. And always by the same method."

"Tell us about the method," Holmes asked.

"The victim was always disembowelled, and then staked up as if it were still alive," Captain Lewellen said, wiping sweat from his red face. "Around it were five stones. And a note on the victim always said, 'Beware of the Five — Stop Construction'."

"How ghastly!" I said. "But what has this to do with double murder?"

"The latest victims were humans," the Captain choked. "Two men — strangers — killed precisely in the same manner."

"When did this occur?" Holmes asked.

"The bodies were discovered at dawn yesterday," the Captain replied. "About one-half mile north of the Exposition grounds. It's beginning to make the work crews quite edgy, needless to say. Since they are working twenty-four hours a day, some crews are coming and going in the middle of the night."

"How frightening," I observed.

"We're afraid that construction is bound to be affected badly," Captain Lewellen sighed. "We are on a very tight schedule. And if this Exposition fails to open on time, I'm afraid that Omaha will be financially ruined forever."

"Did the police preserve the murder scene?" Holmes asked clinically.

"Perfectly," Lewellen assured him. "When I confided to Police Chief Smith that you would be arriving today, he agreed to cooperate fully. The bodies of the poor victims have been preserved with ice for your inspection."

"Excellent," Holmes said. "And though this has nothing to do with the threat against the President, I shall be happy to solve this little crime so that you can continue with your construction apace."

"Little crime?" the Captain exclaimed, his red face literally aglow.

"And just how can you be sure," I asked with amazement, "that this unpleasantness has nothing to do with the McKinley business?"

"Simple deduction, my dear Watson," Holmes said with his usual triumphant patience. "We have several factions to consider. The Spaniards may seek revenge on the President if the Cuban affair turns sour. The Cuban nationals, now threatened by the local insurgents, might plan the

same. The Indian unrest in Minnesota might also be
a factor. Or, countries sympathetic to Spain for one
reason or another, who will be exhibiting wares or
have spies visiting the Exposition, might be planning some mischief against the President just to
upset possible peace negotiations."

"An interesting comment on the world situation," I said. "But what has it to do with the two
murders?"

"Nothing, my dear fellow," Holmes replied
patiently. "All of these parties are quite anxious to
isolate the President far from Washington. He
would be an infinitely easier target in a frontier
setting than in the heavily guarded Nation's capitol."

"So?" I asked.

"So all of the groups that I mentioned would
want the Exposition to be completed on time,"
Holmes replied. "I would be willing to wager that
many of their agents are currently employed on the
construction crews as well, in order to hasten its
completion. No, Watson. Whoever is perpetrating
the nocturnal mutilation is doing so for the purpose
of stopping the Exposition. Tomorrow we will
examine the evidence, and proceed from there. Tell
me, Captain Lewellen, has there ever been any mutilation business in the area before?"

"Now that you mention it, there were several
cases back in 1891 and '92," he mused. "I had just
gotten out of the military, so I wasn't privy to the
details, however."

"Have someone collect the information for me
in the morning, will you?" Holmes requested. "And
now, gentlemen, since the train has started to
move, I must put all of my concentration on the
scenery. This is the route that the President's train

will be travelling when he pays his visit to the Exposition?"

"Precisely," the Captain replied.

"I shall have a list of security precautions for you by tomorrow evening," Holmes said crisply.

If the Captain's and my idle conversation disturbed Holmes during the trip, his rapt concentration on the details of the scenery never showed it. We were interrupted only once. Captain Lewellen went out for a bit, and returned with a somewhat rumpled but preoccupied gentleman.

"He's a bit hard-of-hearing," the Captain said, "so you may have to shout at him a bit."

"Of course," Holmes said, with a look of sheer admiration that was normally quite alien to his nature. "I recognize you, and am delighted to make your acquaintance."

"What's that?" the stranger shouted.

"He's pleased to meet you," the Captain fairly screamed in his ear.

"And I am pleased to meet you, Mr. Sherlock Holmes," the man said. "And you, too, Dr. Watson. I just wanted to assure you that I have thoroughly inspected the electrical plans for the Exposition — and they are truly spectacular —and I'm convinced that they will pose no security threat to the President."

It was not until much later that I learned that the strange visitor to our train compartment was Thomas Alva Edison.

CHAPTER FOUR

The Trans-Mississippi commission had
arranged quarters for us in a large, rather tasteless
brick home north of the downtown area. It was late
in the evening when our hack finally deposited us on
the doorstep of Clara Thoms' boarding house. In the
not-too-far distance, we could distinctly hear the
workmen's hammers, as they pounded through the
clear night air, pushing construction at the Exposition grounds. The proprietress herself responded to
Captain Lewellen's knocking, and admitted us to a
most comfortable parlor. Indeed, the interior of the
building was in such sharp contrast to its drab
exterior, it was difficult for me to believe that it was
the same structure. The faces of three small female
children, one face on top of the other like an Indian
totem pole, peered curiously from a slightly ajar

bedroom door.

"You girls get back in bed now," Mrs. Thoms whispered quietly, as she hied them back into their room, and closed the door. "They're really quite sweet little things," she assured us. "But they are constantly under foot."

"Mrs. Thoms, this is Mr. Sherlock Holmes, and his friend, Dr. John H. Watson," the Captain said by way of introduction. "As we agreed, they will occupy the entire second floor. And you will have no other boarders for the duration of the Exposition."

"That is our agreement, Captain Lewellen," Clara Thoms acknowledged.

"Actually," the Captain continued, "Dr. Watson is your only official guest. Mr. Holmes will of course share his quarters, but he will be in disguise when in public. No one but you, myself, Police Chief Smith, and the Commission directors must know his true identity, or that he is even in the country."

"Considering the rental contribution that the Commission has made on behalf of my poor fatherless daughters," Mrs. Thoms replied, "you can count on my complete cooperation."

Captain Lewellen took his leave, and the widow Thoms preceded us up the stairs, illuminating the way with a candle. Her rather shapeless torso, which was concealed by a dress that greatly resembled a potato sack, blocked a good deal of the candlelight, leaving Holmes and I to negotiate the stairs mostly in the dark.

"Some of the finer Omaha neighborhoods are installing the new electric lights," she explained.

"But it will be a long while before this poor home sees anything but candles and gaslights."

"I assure you that we are quite used to the comfortable conveniences that you afford us, Mrs. Thoms," I said. Holmes took the first room at the head of the stairs, announcing that he would retire immediately.

"And this will be your room, Dr. Watson," she said, as her candle revealed a most comfortable apartment. "Tell me, doctor — is there a Mrs. Watson?"

"Indeed there is," I assured her. "And a finer woman you will never find."

"And lucky to have such a nice husband as you," she replied. "I presume that there is a Mrs. Holmes, as well?"

"If you are referring to my friend's late mother — yes." I chuckled at the thought of Holmes in any kind of domestic situation.

"How very interesting," the widow Thoms reflected. "Goodnight, Dr. Watson. Breakfast is at seven." She shut the door, and left me quite to myself.

"Great heavens," I muttered aloud. "Is Sherlock Holmes about to be approached romantically? I wonder if his finely tuned brain is likely to explode under such pressure."

CHAPTER FIVE

At seven o'clock the next morning, Holmes somewhat reluctantly descended with me to the breakfast table. Holmes had chosen to be disguised as a business executive this first day, and looked very much the part. The widow Thoms must not have slept at all the previous night, so sumptuous was the repast spread before us. Not only were there bacon and eggs, my addiction to which I have previously alluded, but there were rolls and biscuits which the widow personally delivered hot from the oven. There were waffles and juice and toast as well. I was as awed as Holmes was nauseated, as was customary to victims of his addiction.

The widow Thoms had not neglected her own person either. My impression of her the previous evening had been that of a rather plain woman of perhaps forty years of age, with hair pulled back into a bun, and a tent-type dress one normally associates with servants. This morning she was clad in a dress that accented her well endowed physical features. Her hair had been combed out to reveal very long tresses, which were attractively pinned back with sky-blue barrettes that matched her eyes, which now seemed to sparkle.

The three little girls who sat quietly on one side of the breakfast table had more the appearance of occupying a pew in Church than their mother's kitchen. They were dressed in what had to be their Sunday best. And their impeccable behavior throughout the meal suggested all sorts of threatened maternal tortures should their decorum prove anything short of exemplary.

If all of this was for Holmes' benefit, it was a totally wasted effort. He grudgingly consented to a glass of strange looking juice, which he sipped at sporadically while waiting for me. I must confess that I consumed enough to make up for Holmes, and our hack driver was obliged to wait a full ten minutes before Holmes finally persuaded me that there were two murders waiting to be solved.

Captain Lewellen ordered the hack to take us first to the Exposition site. Seeming to use the sounds of hammers and saws as a beacon, the horse quickly trotted a distance of perhaps four city blocks, and through a gate. Instantly we were transported into a world that defied belief.

There lay before us a small city of the utmost grandeur. A lagoon that would have rivaled any in Venice stretched in front of us a full three hundred yards, with a huge fountain spraying water a hundred feet high in all directions. A statue of King Neptune graced the top of the fountain. The lagoon was lined on both sides by luxurious buildings of grand design that would have made Paris proud. Every building was artfully adorned with murals, brocades, moldings, and semi-nude statuary.

Everywhere, workmen crawled over various projects like so many bugs. Hundreds were planting trees, shrubs, and ornate flower gardens. Others employed an army of mules to complete paving projects. One large crew was working to complete an ornate bridge across the center of the lagoon. No bee hive ever could emulate such activity.

"Marvelous," I said breathlessly. "Surely such a wonder took years to create and shall last for a century."

"Neither, I'm afraid," Captain Lewellen laughed. "We're in our fifteenth month of construction, to be completed in two more weeks. And by this time next year, it will be all gone."

"What a waste!" I exclaimed.

"Not really," the Captain said. "Construction is of amazingly cheap quality, considering the effect. Mostly wood, with plaster of Paris providing the decoration. By the time the Exposition closes in five months time, these buildings will already be badly deteriorated."

"Well, Holmes," I asked, "what impresses you the most?"

"I am impressed the most," he replied, "with the thought that these hundreds of workmen of necessity include many of our future adversaries. It shall be great fun tracking each of them down." I should have guessed that such grandeur would not be the object of Sherlock Holmes' single-purposed attention.

"I can take you to the murder scene now," Captain Lewellen said. "Since the Exposition site was on the way, I figured that you might want a quick glance at it."

"Good thinking, too, I might add," Holmes replied absently. He scanned the rows of buildings, first on one side, then the other. As the hack moved through the Exposition grounds and out into the countryside, I had no doubts that although Holmes was unimpressed with the scene, he could accurately reproduce every detail if needed.

The horse trotted at a steady gait for perhaps ten minutes, when we climbed over a small rise and descended into a slight depression that looked rather like a large shallow bowl. The area at the bottom was staked out with ropes, and guarded by three uniformed policemen. We quickly alit, and proceeded to the scene.

"You can dismiss these men," Holmes suggested. "We won't be needing them here anymore." The Captain complied, as Holmes began his usual painstaking inspection of the area. He began his search some fifty feet from the point where the bodies had been found, and circled the site at that distance. For perhaps an hour, he worked his way in increasingly smaller concentric circles. Now and then, he would stoop to examine some detail more closely, often using his magnifying glass. On three occasions, he carefully picked up a small item and placed it in a separate envelope which he pocketed. The Captain and I watched silently, 'til he ultimately arrived at the murder scene itself.

"Are these the actual stakes on which the corpses were propped?" Holmes asked.

"The very ones," the Captain replied.

"We will need them," Holmes said. "And I must compliment your local police for the fine way that they have preserved this scene."

"You'll have your chance to compliment Police Chief Smith yourself presently," Lewellen said. "Just as soon as you are through inspecting the murder scene."

"I'm quite through here," Holmes replied. "But I assure you, this is not the scene of the murders."

We removed the stakes, placed them in the hack, and returned back through the Trans-Mississippi Exposition grounds. As we passed Clara Thoms' boarding house, she waved gaily to us from her large wooden front porch. I waved back, but Sherlock Holmes failed to notice his landlady, or so it appeared.

The street was busy with private carriages, hacks and pedestrians, wending their way amid the streetcars. The horse-drawn versions had all been replaced by the modern motorized cars. As we passed down the bluff, we could see a mass of railroad tracks at its foot, that spread like so many match-sticks almost to the banks of the adjacent Missouri River. We passed through residential areas that ranged from mansions for the very rich to the humblest of abodes. Presently, the driver pulled up in front of a building marked **Police Station**, and we disembarked with our metal stakes.

Holmes complimented Police Chief Smith after proper introductions were complete, and we were then led to view the bodies of the still unidentified victims. They had been packed in crushed ice, and kept in a sealed room.

"Were they nude when you found them?" Holmes asked.

"Just as you see them," Chief Smith replied. "Propped up like a couple of bloodless ghouls. I've investigated many a murder in my time, but I've never witnessed anything this ghastly."

"I fancy not," I replied. But Holmes was already examining the corpses, as calmly and unperturbed as I might inspect a patient's tonsils. His demeanor struck the rest of us dumb, as he silently completed his inspection.

"Once again, I compliment you on the fine job you have done in preserving evidence," Holmes said sincerely. "It greatly simplifies my work."

"How you can describe this case as simple mystifies me," Chief Smith said.

"I understand that similar animal mutilations occurred in the earlier part of the decade," Holmes said.

"Yes," Chief Smith replied. "I've gathered the police reports, as well as a few newspaper articles concerning them."

The documents were placed before Holmes, who quickly but carefully scanned them.

"Hello. What's this?" Holmes exclaimed, as he came upon an item that captured his attention. "So, part of the Exposition site was once used as a race track."

"That's true," the Chief said. "Back in '92 and '93. But the Depression did it in, along with just about everything else. The Exposition is about all that really put Omaha back on its feet."

"When did the race track close?" Holmes inquired.

"That's an easy one," Chief Smith smiled. "September 1, 1893. It was my birthday — and I won twenty dollars."

"Interesting," Holmes mused. "Very interesting."

At that moment, a police sergeant entered the room.

"We have a break in the double-murder case, Chief," the man announced. "We need you in the next room."

"Perhaps your services weren't required after all, Sherlock Holmes," the Chief remarked.

"Perhaps," Holmes said with a slight smile. "May we be permitted to join you?"

"Of course," the Chief replied. "I would want it no other way."

We entered a large room that contained as unlikely a collection of people as I could imagine. Besides an assortment of policemen, both uniformed and plain-clothed, there were two robed monks, one of which carried a firearm. There was also a strange group which consisted of a gaggle of five cringing people, including three bearded men with wide-brimmed hats, plus two women wearing strange bonnets that were most out of style with the times.

"Aha," Holmes said with exultation. "You must be the five 'Children of Adam'. What fortunate luck!"

"Fortunate indeed," the sergeant replied. "Thanks to these two civic-minded monks, our double-murder has been solved."

"I totally agree," Holmes said.

"You see," the taller monk said, "one of our brothers was meditating during a private retreat in the wilderness north of the Exposition grounds night before last. From a safe distance, he watched these five members of that unwholesome cult butcher those unfortunate men. Since he was one of our older more feeble members, there was no way he could have safely intervened, without being martyred on a stake himself. He reported the incident to me immediately, however."

"We do not take human life," the older woman wept. "It is totally against our religious principles. The animals were our property."

"I confess," the armed monk continued, "that our group has been much too separated from this community, sealing ourselves off in our monastery. However, with the advent of the Trans-Mississippi Exposition, we have determined to become an active sector of the City."

"About time, I might add," Captain Lewellen interjected.

"It struck me that we might show the community our intentions by capturing this dastardly group," the monk said, "and turning them over to the police for what hopefully will be speedy justice."

"Good thinking," Chief Smith said enthusiastically.

"A while back," the monk continued, "a man with an unfortunate background asked to join our order. When he was accepted, he turned this gun over to me, which I assure you I detest. But last night, I removed it from its hiding place, and together with Brother Merrill set out to catch these wicked people in the act. At about three o'clock this morning, approximately a half mile west of the Exposition grounds, we apprehended them in the act of eviscerating and staking this rabbit, in the same manner as those unfortunate men were murdered the night before."

"The animals we killed," the elder of the group admitted. "But not the men."

"A likely story," Chief Smith said. "Sergeant, lock them up until they can be formally charged with their crimes."

As the wretched group was being led away, Holmes stepped forward, and said, "I am truly impressed, Brother —?"

"Gregory," the happy monk replied. "And my companion is Brother Merrill."

"Brother Gregory," Holmes went on. "This is a most singular service you have made to our community. As one of the wealthier contributors to the Exposition, I wish to reward your order handsomely."

"Please, good sir," the monk protested. "We have taken the vow of poverty." It struck me that Brother Merrill's face dropped a bit.

"But if it's your purpose to have a new relationship with the community," Holmes pushed on, "surely a nest-egg of say one thousand dollars would permit you to do all sorts of good deeds for the needy of the area without breaking your most noble vow of poverty." I could perhaps have been mistaken, but Brother Merrill seemed to nudge Brother Gregory ever so slightly.

"Well," Brother Gregory mused, "if we used it purely for charity, I suppose that God would not only understand but perhaps approve. Very well, good sir, on behalf of the poor, I accept your generous offer."

"I will go to my bank this afternoon," Holmes said, as I watched more than a little baffled, "and will deliver it to your monastery this evening. I trust that your cloister is well-guarded and requires a password."

"Our cloister changes the password daily," Brother Gregory replied. "As a most pure practice of religion, we don't dare permit the possibility of contamination."

"If I am to deliver your well-deserved thousand dollar reward — after all, by saving the Exposition, you have saved me ten times that much — I shall need today's password," Holmes said calmly.

"Of course," Brother Gregory replied. "But you must deliver it prior to ten o'clock this evening, because that is when tomorrow's password takes effect. Simply say, 'I have the keys to the kingdom', and the lookout will pass you through the gate. God bless you, my son."

After the monks had left, I exclaimed, "What in heaven's name was that all about?"

"How dare you play such games with those brave men of the cloth," Chief Smith sputtered.

"Have some of your strongest plain-clothes police officers follow them," Holmes instructed. "Tell them to be extremely cautious, because these men are exceedingly dangerous. When they are certain that our frocked friends have both hands out from under their cassocks, they are to overpower them, disarm them, and return them to us. Hurry, man, before they get away."

Although somewhat confused, the Chief obeyed Holmes, nevertheless. After dispatching a group of civilian clad policemen, he said, "I certainly hope that you know what you're doing, Holmes. I have the feeling that after this, that group of monks will never venture out into this community again."

"I daresay you are right," Holmes agreed. "While we're waiting for your husky detectives to return, you might bring that unfortunate group of religious zealots to our presence."

"But — we're holding them for murder," the Chief said.

"If murdering a doe rabbit is a capital offense in the State of Nebraska," Holmes observed dryly, "then charge them. I assure you that they are guilty of nothing more. However, I do believe that they need to be remonstrated somewhat for their disrupting effects on the Trans-Mississippi Exposition, which I am more and more convinced is a most important project."

The "Children of Adam" were duly chastised, and after promising no more disrupting tactics toward the Exposition, were permitted to leave, agreeing not to leave the area until all of this unpleasantness was ultimately resolved.

Presently, the burly plain-clothed policemen returned with the two "Brothers" in custody.

"Unfrock them," Holmes ordered. "Not that they were ever worthy of wearing their robes. Chief Smith, may I present you two of the murderers of your unknown victims who are presently iced down in the next room."

"You mean," I gasped, "there are more murderers?"

"Five more," Holmes said confidently. "How heavily were they armed?" he asked one of the arresting policemen.

"Each had two revolvers," the man replied. "Fully loaded."

"I suspected as much," Holmes said. "Under their cassocks, they had all four levelled at your policemen the entire time they were here — just in case their plot failed. That's why I didn't have you arrest them on the spot."

"But — how in the world did you ever suspect them?" I asked in astonishment. "They certainly looked and talked convincingly."

"Suspect is the wrong terminology, Watson," Holmes said with conviction. "As you know, I have long been a student of religious practices — not because of any supernatural beliefs of my own, which of course I don't possess. But rather because crimes are often committed in the name of righteousness. And the tenets of each sect bear their own footprints, as surely as a plaster cast of such an imprint can identify its owner."

"Then you were familiar with these so-called 'Children of Adam'?" Captain Lewellen asked.

"Only through the literature," Holmes replied. "They are a small agrarian sect, who believe that evil spirits roam the world, corrupting as they go. These spirits can only be dispelled if 'clean spirits' are set loose to fight them. Their belief that all animal spirits are 'clean' leads them to the practice of aiming an animal toward the evil place, and therefore at the 'evil spirits' as well, and then liberating its spirit. The 'clean spirit' then drives the 'evil spirit' to another part of the world, thereby making the immediate area safe if only for a time."

"How in heaven's name could anyone believe such poppycock?" I asked, with no small measure of disgust.

"Why not?" Holmes replied. "After all, it worked in 1892 and '93. These same folk set the animal spirits free to fight the 'evil' race track spirit. And, notwithstanding the world-wide depression, of which these simple agrarian folk were probably never aware, they undoubtedly believed that their cult practice had been successful."

"But — who are the murder victims?" Chief Smith asked, without shame admitting that he was not the equal to Sherlock Holmes.

"Former accomplices of our 'Brothers', Holmes stated firmly. "If you re-examine the corpses, you will note a faint but recognizable callous ring about both victims ankles — the same type of calluses I detected beneath the robes of 'Brothers' Merrill and Gregory. As Watson will undoubtedly assure you, I make it a point to keep track of crime world-wide, through copious reading of newspaper reports."

"Quite true," I confirmed.

"I was aware that a chain-gang in the State of Georgia overpowered and killed their guards last year," Holmes went on. "There were twelve of them altogether. One was killed outright by a guard prior to his own demise. Two others were victims of the swamp area they escaped through — one by disease, the other in an alligator's jaws. The other nine have not been heard from since. Simple mathematics tell us that by subtracting 'Brothers' Gregory and Merrill, as well as the two victims themselves, we still have five desperadoes with which to deal at the cloister."

"You'll never take them alive," Gregory hissed at Holmes. "And you can be sure that they'll kill a score of you in the attempt — not to mention the monks as well."

"That confirms my conclusion that the true monks are still alive," Holmes nodded. "But obviously you had intended to murder them after your adventure was complete."

"You can't prove that," Merrill growled.

"The facts speak for themselves," Holmes stated. "Two of your group, who undoubtedly had some religious background in spite of their criminal lives, balked at the cold-blooded killing of innocent holy men."

"Pure conjecture," Gregory sneered.

"Something had to be done with them," Holmes continued. "Also, something had to be done about the people who were mutilating animals around the Exposition grounds in an effort to frighten the workmen off the job. After all, a great deal of profit hinged on the Exposition opening on schedule and remaining open for a long period of time."

"Please continue," Chief Smith commented, with open admiration for the great detective.

"Then 'Brother' Gregory came up with an ingenius plan to solve both problems with one stroke," Holmes said. "And it very nearly worked. It was undoubtedly a small problem for his hoodlums to track down the simple 'Children of Adam', and observe their primitive animal sacrifices. After all, these men had spent the greater part of their lives living in the shadows of society themselves. Their scheme was to murder their two dissenting comrades, and to make it appear as if the animal mutilators had graduated to human victims, as is too often the sad truth."

"But — where did they give themselves away?" Captain Lewellen queried.

"In any number of ways," Holmes replied. "First, the victims were human, which would be utterly abhorable to the 'Children of Adam'. Second, the victims were obviously murdered elsewhere — at the cloister, I presume — due to the lack of blood at the scene of such obvious carnage. Third, if you examine that unfortunate doe rabbit that the 'Brothers' so helpfully supplied, you'll find that its jugular vein was opened prior to the evisceration. A careful examination of yesteryear's newspapers, as well as the current animal victims, will show the same was true of all the current animal sacrifices. 'Children of Adam' believe that blood contains the animal's spirit, hence it must be released en toto if it is to be effective against the 'evil' spirits. The throats of our two human victims were quite intact, one more evidence that the 'Children of Adam' had not graduated to human sacrifice. Fourth, by the positions of the stakes — which were metal, by the way, not the required wood — by the positions of the stakes that supported our human scarecrows, there was no possible way that both victims could be facing the Exposition grounds, a positive must for any 'Children of Adam' sacrifice. Fifth, all 'Children of Adam' sacrifices, as evidenced by the gender of our unfortunate rabbit, of necessity must be female. I could go on and on, thanks to the sheer stupidity of our helpful but phoney 'Brothers'."

"By Prince Albert's beard, Holmes," I exclaimed, "I will never cease to be amazed at your abilities."

"But — what made you suspect the 'Brothers'," Chief Smith wanted to know.

"Some fifty feet from the discovery site of the bodies, I found a small cross," Holmes related. "As unlikely as it seemed that a member of the cloth might be a participant in homicide, I could hardly discount the possibility. A strange black button was located some twenty feet from the carnage, which you will note, not only perfectly matches those on the 'Brothers' garbs, but appears to be the very one

missing from 'Brother' Gregory's sleeve. The faint
but undeniable footprint of a sandal in a fortunate
bit of mud confirmed my theory, since my study of
the subject concluded that it was worn exclusively by
clerics. I'll be happy to send you a copy of the paper
that I have written on the subject."

"I'd be obliged," Chief Smith replied.

"But what of the fate of the unfortunate true
Brothers at the cloister?" I asked.

"They are doomed," Gregory screamed at us.

"Thanks to 'Brothers' Gregory and Merrill,"
Holmes said amiably, "the fortunes of the true
Brothers are about to improve.'"

"Whoever you are," Gregory hissed, "I curse
the day you were born."

"Pity that you shall never know the identity of
your nemesis," I allowed. "Perhaps then you would
not feel quite so badly at being exposed."

"Lock these men up, Chief Smith," Holmes
said. "We have until ten o'clock tonight to secure
the release of the true Brothers, and to capture the
remaining five murderers."

CHAPTER SIX

Never in my wildest imagination would I have dreamed the adventure that Sherlock Holmes and I were about to experience. I now detail the events of the evening of June 10th, 1898, as I vividly recall them.

We left the police station at dusk, accompanied by Chief Smith and a dozen of his finest officers. About an hour after sunset, Chief Smith ordered the contingent into a darkened grove.

"This is as close as we can get without being sighted by their look-out," he announced. "From the top of the hill in front of us, you will be able to see the cloister across the valley."

"Thank you, my friend," Holmes replied. "If all goes according to plan, we shall meet with you within the hour."

"I still wish that you would permit one of my men to go in your stead," Chief Smith wagged his head. "Or at the very least accompany you."

"Unfortunately, none of your men possesses my talent for imitating voices," Holmes reminded him. "Nor do any of them match the height and shape of 'Brother Merrill' as well as Watson."

"I beg your pardon," I said, somewhat offended.

"In any case," Holmes went on, "I could not feel more safe with any companion, considering the adventures that we have been through together. Right, Watson?"

"Quite right," I agreed, my ego totally restored.

"Well, gentlemen, the moon appears to be illuminating the valley," Holmes said with unbridled enthusiasm. "So it is time for our departure. Do you have your revolver, Watson?"

"Of course," I replied. "And you?"

"Fully loaded," Holmes smiled, "as well as the handcuffs that Chief Smith was good enough to supply."

Holmes and I made a strange sight indeed, as we stepped into the bright moonlit meadow, wrapped in the robes that had previously been the attire of 'Brothers' Gregory and Merrill respectively.

"I say, Holmes," I exclaimed. "I don't know whether to feel frightened or foolish in this outlandish costume. Heaven forbid that I should meet my maker clothed as I am now."

"I assure you, your maker will have some time to wait before he greets you, Watson. Take care not to step on your robe, or you will go down like a shot."

"You seem quite confident of your plan," I said, lifting the front of my robe slightly as we crossed the crest of the hill. Suddenly there loomed before us, perched on the opposite hill, a large old structure reminiscent of a medieval European castle. In the bright moonlight, we could clearly see the huge stone wall that surrounded the main building. Turrets stood out at each corner of the structure, which appeared to be constructed of some sort of gray stone.

"Behold, the cloister," Holmes announced.

"They seem to have forgotten the moat and drawbridge," I said dryly.

"Hardly a necessity," Holmes commented. "With the view it commands, no one could get closer than a half mile without being seen. Aha! We have been spotted already."

"We have? How can you be sure?" I asked.

"A reflection at the front gate — answered by another in the north turret," Holmes explained. "See? It was just repeated."

"Oh yes," I said. "I believe that I did catch a glimpse of something."

"They have undoubtedly been wondering about Gregory and Merrill's mission," Holmes said, as we descended into the valley that separated us from the monastery. "They have probably been worried about such a late return. My guess is that the sentry at the gate signalled an accomplice in the turret of our return, and that the accomplice in turn is informing the other three of the same information."

"I hope for the sake of our futures that your guess is correct," I said, gripping my trusty revolver under my cassock. Presently we were climbing the hill toward the cloister. When we were perhaps thirty feet from the wall, a voice from the guard-house just behind the gate demanded to know who we were.

"Brother Gregory and Brother Merrill," Holmes shouted back. I was positively astounded. If I had not been certain that the man beside me was indeed Sherlock Holmes, I would have sworn that "Brother" Gregory had somehow escaped, so closely did Holmes imitate his voice. "I have the keys to the kingdom," Holmes added, reciting the password that would certainly gain us our entrance. Immediately we heard the clanking sound of a large key turning a lock. A heavily armed sentry greeted us, as the iron gate swung open.

"Where have you two been?" the man asked. Per Holmes' plan, we remained silent as we approached the sentry. "Did everything go well?" the sentry asked hopefully. "Is something wrong?"

"Wounded," Holmes muttered in Gregory's voice, then collapsed to his knees, making certain to keep the guardhouse between us and the main building.

"Oh, my god," the sentry said, laying his firearm aside. As he bent to assist Holmes, I laid the barrel of my revolver against the back of his head.

"One sound," I threatened, "and you will have a gaping hole where your brain used to be."

"What is this?" the sentry whispered. "Why — you're not Gregory or Merrill!"

"Nor am I wounded," Holmes replied, deftly handcuffing the sentry's hands behind him. "Before we gag you, I am giving you the opportunity of providing us with information regarding the locations of your colleagues as well as that of the monks you now hold prisoner."

"Why should I do that?" the man sneered.

"Perhaps to save your from an appointment

with the hangman," I replied, "for being cooperative."

"I'll hang in any case," the man said in despair. "For it was our plan to murder the true Brothers as soon as Gregory and Merrill returned."

"Great heavens!" I exclaimed.

"I am afraid," Holmes said, "that we shall have to perform the rescue without the benefit of Chief Smith's gendarmes, Watson."

"It wasn't my idea," the wicked wretch moaned. "But the monks have become a problem. Just this morning, two of the younger ones nearly escaped."

"How so?" I asked.

"We don't know. The monks are securely imprisoned in an underground cell," the man said. "Then, quite by surprise, they appeared at the gate, overpowered the sentry, and were over the next hill before we caught them. If they had gotten away, everything would be over for us."

"So," I said with measured disgust, "you voted to murder these men of God." It occurred to me that Holmes was prowling the interior of the guard-house, his full attention intensely focused on each stone, one by one. "I say," I enquired, "just what is it that you are looking for, Holmes?"

"If you were the architect of such a monstrous atrocity as this building, Watson," Holmes asked, "where would you conceal the entrance to a secret tunnel in this room?"

"I have no idea, Holmes," I replied with a shrug. "Perhaps this fellow could be of some help to us."

"Not a chance," Holmes said, his great mind still obviously attempting to invade the mind of the long-dead designer of the monastery. "Of course," he finally concluded. "It's really so logical. Hand me the gate key, Watson." Holmes took the key and inserted it into what appeared to be a chink in the mortar between two large stones. Immediately, a stone that was as large as a horse swung slowly outward on a hidden hinge.

"Great Scott!" I exclaimed.

"Gregory! Merrill! Michael!" an impatient voice shouted from the doorway of the cloister itself. "What in the world is detaining you?"

"One moment," Holmes voice once again duplicated that of "Brother" Gregory. "I'm telling our friend Michael the good news."

"Then your mission was successful?" the voice shouted out.

"Totally," Holmes replied. Then, in a hushed voice, he said, "Quick, Watson! Into the passage-way. Gag our friend Michael, and take him with you."

"What are you up to, Holmes?" I asked, quickly following his directions.

"No time to explain," Holmes replied. "Just wait inside until I come to you," The huge stone door swung shut, and Michael and I might just as well have been entombed, it was so dark in the tunnel. I was suddenly panicked totally, as confined spaces are most fearsome to me. From this vantage point, I could distinctly hear Holmes play out his scenario.

"Help! Help!" I heard him shout, once again using "Brother" Gregory's voice. "He's trying to escape."

I then heard two unfamiliar voices shout "Who?" "Who is trying to escape?"

"It's Michael," Holmes replied. "He told me that he would have no part in killing the monks, and said that he would prefer to run for his life. Brother Merrill is chasing him up over the hill. I would have given chase as well, but Michael injured my leg with the butt of his gun."

"This is too much," the first voice said. "You two go help Merrill catch that coward. Bring him back, and he'll taste the same fate facing the monks. Go quickly."

"I'll guard the gate until they return," I heard Holmes say. Moments later, the great stone door once again swung open, and I took a long gulp of badly needed fresh air.

"Well, Watson," Holmes said triumphantly, "those two should be in for quite a surprise when they dash over the hill into Chief Smith's arms. Quickly, now, we have two more murderers to apprehend."

So saying, he stepped into the tunnel, and swung the great stone door shut, once again leaving us in total darkness.

"Holmes," I said, with no small degree of terror, "you know that I suffer hopelessly from claustrophobia. Isn't there some other way of gaining entrance to this wretched building?"

"Curing yourself of that bothersome condition has been long since overdue," Holmes replied through the darkness. "Come, take my hand, old fellow. I shall be your guide." Holmes grabbed my hand, and led me down the tunnel at a speed that made me nearly forget my fear of being buried alive. The man was uncanny. He might just as well have been a cat that could see equally well in total darkness as in the daylight. We moved for what seemed miles, with me imagining that we were plunging ever hopelessly into the bowels of the earth. Suddenly

Holmes stopped, and at the same time, I thought that my heart would stop. My eyes began playing tricks on me, for I thought that I could see a crack of light in front of me. Then I heard a strange voice say, "Good Lord, the devils have discovered the hidden passageway."

"We're friends," Holmes replied. "We have come to rescue you, Pray help me to open this stubborn door." In an instant, the tunnel was flooded with light from the lamps that lit the cell in front of us.

"Who are you?" a hooded figure asked.

"We're friends, just as I said," Holmes replied. "And I regret to say that you and your comrades are in great danger."

"We're quite aware of that," the monk replied. "And we are also quite prepared to be martyred."

"That won't be necessary," Holmes informed him. "How many of you are there?"

"Eleven," the monk replied. At that moment, we could hear a key turning in the cell door.

"Quickly," Holmes ordered. "Two of you get into the tunnel, and close the entrance." The act was completed just as the two remaining scoundrels entered the cell, one armed with a pistol, the other with a large knife very much like a machete.

"We need two volunteers," the one man said.

Holmes aged his voice by forty years, and replied, "I'm old, and have few years left in any case. I choose to volunteer. And my life-long friend here will volunteer as well."

"Very well," the man replied. "Come with us." With their weapons trained on us, we left the cell, which they promptly locked behind us. We were led down a series of corridors, and into a dimly lit cell that contained what appeared to be a butcher's block.

"You have a choice," the man with the revolver announced. "You can either be impaled with the knife or beheaded. Which will it be?"

"Dear me," Holmes said in mocked confusion, still using his aged man's voice. "The main reason that I joined the monastery was because I hated to make decisions."

"Very well," the man said. "Then I shall make it for you." He forced Holmes head down on the block, and said, "Do you have any last words?"

"As a matter of fact, I do," Holmes replied weakly. Then added, in his own voice, "Unless you wish to be dead men, lay down your weapons at once."

"What?" the man with the knife said with a sneer.

"Unless you are quite blind," Holmes said, raising his head from the block, "you will note that my friend has two revolvers aimed at your heads. I assure you that his marksmanship is of the highest order."

When Police Chief Smith and his entourage arrived at the appointed hour, they found our three prisoners handcuffed to the front gate.

"I'm sorry to have kept you gentlemen up so late," Holmes greeted them. "It appears that we did not need your assistance after all. By the by, the people in charge of the mining exhibit for the State of Oregon will undoubtedly be interested in the return of this package. It contains a gold ingot and a silver ingot, the combined value of which is about thirty thousand dollars."

CHAPTER SEVEN

It was just past ten o'clock when Police Chief Smith dropped us at our boarding house. The widow Thoms had the front door open even as we alit from our carriage.

"Welcome home, Dr. Watson," she shouted gaily from the porch. "And how nice of Sherlock Holmes to make a call on me once again."

"He lives here," I reminded her, though my words did not seem to penetrate her consciousness. She showed us to the parlor, where we gratefully accepted her offer of a cup of tea and two most comfortable chairs. "You know, Holmes," I said, "you will never cease to amaze me. We have been here only four and twenty hours, and already you have solved what is probably the most baffling case ever to hit this frontier town."

"Actually, it was quite simple, my dear Watson," Holmes replied. "The real challenges lay ahead — when President McKinley pays his visit."

"Perhaps the President won't come, the war and all," I surmised. "The morning paper reports that he will present an address to the opening day visitors by telephone, then press a button in Washington that will start the Exposition machinery going. Perhaps that will suffice for him."

"You will also note that the same paper made mentions of thousands of newspaper reporters being transported to Omaha free of charge to cover the Exposition," Holmes reminded me. "Politics being what they are, and with the Congressional elections coming in November, the President will most assuredly come to Omaha. My guess is some time in the middle of October. The publicity resulting from such a trip will be too much of a political temptation."

"Not to change the subject," I said, "but how did you know that our phoney monks possessed the precious gold and silver ingots?" At that moment, Mrs. Thoms' three small daughters came bounding from their bedroom. The widow returned from the kitchen with our tea, and scolded them.

"Girls, get back to bed this instant! Can't you see that Mama has a gentleman caller?"

I winced, but Holmes didn't seem to notice. For all of his ability to deduce truth from obscure details, when it comes to the emotion of love, he is a true dunce.

"I wasn't certain that I would find gold or silver as such," Holmes replied. "But I knew that it would be something of great value."

"But how did it get into their possession?" I queried.

"As you undoubtedly noticed during our brief visit to the Exposition grounds today, there were a great many men employed in a variety of activities."

"What of it?" I asked.

"It would appear that anyone who wants to work will be hired," Holmes said, "with no inquiry as to his character. One or more of our priestly friends undoubtedly held legitimate construction jobs, and kept an eye on valuable shipments coming in. When the receipt for delivery of those ingots is located, the name will be fictitious, but the handwriting you can be sure will match that of "Brother" Gregory.

"Marvelous!" I said.

"Yes, our greedy criminals had a good thing going for them," Holmes remarked. "They took over the cloister by having one of their group admitted as a penitent. The first night, he opened the gate to his compatriots, and the true monks have been prisoners ever since."

"And who would suspect monks of being criminals?" I asked. Then added, "Except for Sherlock Holmes."

"I'm afraid you over-estimate me, my friend," Holmes protested. "This group was bold and vicious — and also possessed a certain amount of cunning. But their mentality was basically that of the oaf."

"Sometimes I wonder why we have kept your presence here a secret," I ventured. "If the foreign powers who plan to do President McKinley injustice knew you were here, they probably would change their minds quite readily."

"This time I'm afraid that you under-estimate our potential adversaries," Holmes chided, me. "If Spain, Cuba or another foreign country opts for some sort of revenge, we will be contending with well-trained, well-organized teams of agents who will undoubtedly be willing to sacrifice their lives if necessary to achieve their purposes. And, incidentally, my purpose of the moment is to retire. Goodnight, my friend."

"Goodnight, Mr. Holmes," Mrs. Thoms said cheerfully. Holmes made no reply as he quickly climbed the stairs. "You know, Dr. Watson," she prattled on, "I do believe that your friend has taken a liking to me."

Once again, I winced openly, then made my way to my own sleeping quarters.

CHAPTER EIGHT

Next morning, I arrived at the breakfast table ahead of both Holmes and the widow's chattering offspring. I confess to a mild aversion to small children. Holmes, of course, utterly detests them. I gratefully sat down to what would hopefully be a quiet breakfast and a perusal of the morning paper.

"There was a good deal of excitement yesterday out at the old monastery," Mrs. Thoms informed me, as she deposited my usual breakfast in front of me.

"Do tell," I replied, opening the paper to the front page. "Well, it's refreshing to see that the Americans are equal to England in one capacity."

"And what would that be, my dear Watson?" Holmes asked, as he entered the kitchen.

"Great heavens," I exclaimed. "What kind of a costume is that? I hardly recognize you in that garb."

"Precisely the idea," he said cheerily. "Today I apply for a job as a common laborer at the Exposition grounds."

"Come now, man," I said in disbelief. "We can't be that hard-pressed for funds."

"But we are hard-pressed for information, old fellow. What better way of getting behind the scenes without arousing suspicion. Now, what is in the morning paper worthy of your remark?"

"The report on the events at the cloister," I replied. "Lestrade seems modest by comparison. Listen to these headlines. *'Police Chief Smith Captures Murderers. Brilliant Detective Work. Recovers Valuable Metals. Mayor Moores Praises Chief Smith's Courage.'* And on ad infinitum."

"Well, he could hardly have given credit where it was due, now could he?" Holmes commented amiably. To my astonishment, he then consumed a piece of toast spread with jam. Nor did it escape the fond eyes of our hostess. After Holmes left on foot for the quarter of a mile walk to seek employment, the widow Thoms commented, "Love is a good prescription for an ailing apetite. True, Doctor?" I didn't bother to look up from my newspaper.

With the Exposition opening day a scant three weeks away, Holmes and I fell into something of a routine. Holmes would appear at the breakfast table in his current disguise, much to the amusement of the Thoms toddlers, whom I had dubbed "The Giggle Sisters". To my great pleasure, Holmes' mood remained quite good, and his consumption of food increased steadily. This was undoubtedly due partly to his unaccustomed flirtation with manual labor, but most certainly meant that his great brain was so sufficiently challenged by the case at hand that he was no longer injecting his insidious seven percent solution of cocaine. The widow Thoms, however, attributed his increased interest in her cooking to quite another matter.

After breakfast and Holmes' departure, I would finish the morning paper, then report to my desk. I would complete my journal notes of the previous day's events, and write a long letter to my beloved Mary, who I missed increasingly with each passing day. Then I would work on my speech to open the Homeopath Convention.

Day after day, the morning paper was filled with advertisements of the most preposterous kind. Medicines, presumably developed by prominent practicing physicians, assured a cure for every disease and condition known to man. One edition alone advertised seven different medications, each of which promised to cure syphilis, liver ailments, catarrh, baldness, ague, impotence ("Regain your manhood", seemed to be the key phrase), and consumption. Since I had been given a free choice of subject matters, I determined to inspire my colleagues to rise up as one and rid this budding nation of such charlatans. I wrote a most brilliant and scathing discourse, I must say, that I personally felt would guarantee my place in medical literature. However, when Dr. Farnham, the convention chairman, read it, I thought he would surely have apoplexy. It seems that these "medicines" were not only large financial supporters of the Exposition, but that many of the "discoverers" of these remarkable concoctions were indeed practicing physicians who would be in my audience. I began to question how much of an honor it would be for me to address such a group. But Dr. Farnham assured me that the vast majority of those in attendance were truly great physicians. For the sake of a non-violent convention, I was persuaded to seek a less controversial subject for my oratory.

Holmes would return from his day's labor, always enthusiastic. This somewhat amazed me, since it seemed that he was learning very little. When I pointed this fact of life out to him, his enthusiastic reply would be, "There's the point. I tell you, the air is fairly charged with electricity, not with just the excitement of rushing to complete history's largest World's Fair. Incidentally, no one at the moment is trying to sabotage it. But one can feel intrigue. At the very least, I know that advance agents for many nations are present. Yet, they are so professional, that the moment I isolate one of them, he disappears and another takes his place." He rubbed his hands together in immense glee. "I tell you, Watson! This promises to be a case worthy of all my varied talents." Modesty has never been one of Sherlock Holmes' virtues.

Holmes worked the seven-in-the-morning till three-in-the-afternoon shift the first week, then switched to the three-to-eleven shift the second week. In his varying disguises, he managed to work at every known construction trade. He was paid good wages — thirty cents per hour when he was a carpenter or painter — at the end of each day, which permitted him to change identities on a day-to-day basis. However, since the Exposition commissioners had agreed to use only union workers, most of his wages went for union dues for each of his many aliases. By the end of his second week on the job, he still had failed to uncover any solid clues. However, with what appeared to me to be each succeeding failure, Holmes became increasingly exhilarated. Somehow, he sensed that the challenge continued to grow.

Each evening, Holmes would bring me up-to-date on the events at the Exposition grounds, which I, in turn, have dutifully recorded in my journals. For example, Holmes was particularly fascinated with what seemed to me a somewhat mundane matter. "Today," Holmes said, "a crew of workmen began construction on a new railroad siding, immediately adjacent to the Exposition grounds."

"Do tell," I muttered idly over my newspaper.

"It is, I am told, an accommodation for the extremely wealthy," he continued, not the least non-plussed by my total lack of enthusiasm. "It seems that many of America's richest own their own rail-road cars, which have been sumptuously fitted as veritable mansions on wheels."

"Sounds like a waste of money, if you ask me," I observed.

"Many are planning to visit the Exposition this summer," Holmes went on, "and will actually dwell in these cars just outside the gates. This is positively intriguing."

"If you say so," I replied.

I now began to receive daily letters from my sweet Mary, which buoyed my spirits as well. Still I struggled to find an appropriate topic for my key-note speech to the Homeopath Convention. June 19th at first had seemed a long time distant. With each passing day, my inability to settle on a proper subject brought on an increased feeling of panic.

About a week before opening day, I was sitting in the parlor, grappling with a medical review, when Mrs. Thoms joined me. I had been feeling a bit out of sorts. The widow Thoms began prating for what promised to be the entire evening, driving me quite literally to the edge of insanity. Between my feeling of ague, and the following conversation, I was indeed driven to an early bedtime.

"I do believe that your companion, Mr. Sherlock Holmes, is growing quite fond of me, don't you agree, Dr. Watson?"

"So you seem to believe," I muttered, desperately trying to grasp the nub of the article in an effort to see if it would be an appropriate topic for my speech.

"I love a strong reserved type of man, I must say," she went on. "My late husband was much the same way. By the way, his name was also John — the same as yours."

"What a delightful coincidence," I observed, secretly envying the late John's distinct advantage of not being present.

"My late husband, God rest his soul," she rattled on, once again making me lose my place in the article, "would on occasion accuse me of talking too much, if you can imagine that."

"I believe that my imagination is capable of envisioning such a circumstance," I assured her. "Pray, what was it that caused your deceased husband's demise?"

"It was very odd," she replied, pursing her eyebrows. "He was complaining that if I didn't stop my rambling, he would have to do something desperate. And then he collapsed and died, right there in the chair which you now occupy."

"He was certainly a man of his word," I observed. "And so am I. I do not feel too well myself, Mrs. Thoms. So I think I shall turn in a bit early."

Better that, I thought, than risk the late John Thoms' solution to the problem.

Holmes arrived home, as was his custom about 11:30 P.M., his shift having ended at eleven. Contrary to his usual custom of going directly to bed himself, he proceeded to my bedside and awakened me.

"We finally had a bit of mystery this afternoon," he announced, "and I wanted to make certain that it was not omitted from your journal."

I struggled to my feet, and turned up my lamp. I still felt a bit aching, and was not well-oriented, but sensed that Holmes was in high humor. For a brief moment, I felt that he had spent most of the evening at the corner pub. "What is it, Holmes?" I asked, reaching for my quill. "The Cubans? The Spaniards?"

"Neither," Holmes replied. "It was the Salvation Army!"

"I beg your pardon?" I said, believing that I was in the midst of a bad dream.

"At about five o'clock this afternoon," Holmes said, "there was a terrible commotion near the Illinois building. Thinking that something overt was finally occurring, I, of course, ran to the scene. It seems that two female officers of the Salvation Army had become offended by some of the features of the semi-nude statuary. Sensing a lack of working activity in the area, they used a make-shift ladder to scale the security fence. By the time I arrived on the scene, they had quite defaced one statue, and were busily working on another with heavy hammers."

"You awakened me from my peaceful slumber to tell me this?" I asked somewhat foggily. "Why?"

"Thank God you weren't present, my friend," Holmes said, his hand reassuringly patting my shoulder. "It was not a pretty sight. Knowing your sensitivity to the skillful dissection of the human anatomy, you would have been utterly horrified at the crude destruction these uniformed ladies wrought on certain sensitive and unmentionable organs of those unfortunate statues."

"Holmes," I replied, "I truly believe that hard labor has softened your brain cells." However, since few events amuse Sherlock Holmes, I feel duty bound to include the above notes in my journal, as tasteless as they may appear to the average reader.

With only one week left till the grand opening day of the great Trans-Mississippi and International Exposition, Holmes decided once again to change not only his identity, but his workshift as well.

"Perhaps my quarry moves nocturnally," he said. "In any case, this last week I shall be working from eleven at night until seven in the morning. I have decided to return to the painting of buildings, which seems to be my chief construction talent."

We visited for some time in Mrs. Thoms' parlor, reminiscing about our many mysterious cases, and our long and close friendship. Just as Holmes was about to leave for his new work shift, he paused at the door and said, "You know, my friend, I cannot tell you how happy I am to have met a person who I am assured will be my life-long companion." So saying, he went out the door, headed for another eight hours of painting and sleuthing. As the door closed, I suddenly became aware of a slight moaning behind me. I turned around to observe the widow Thoms, swooning on the floor, appearing indeed to have followed the example of her late husband.

"Mrs. Thoms," I shouted, as I rushed to her side. A quick examination proved that she had only fainted. Presently she came around enough to mutter a few words.

"Be still, my heart." she whispered.

"I assure you," I told her, patting her cheeks back to color, "that your heart is perfectly sound, Mrs. Thoms."

"Doctors!" Mrs. Thoms said with a frown. "Totally insensitive!"

"Insensitive to what?" I asked in astonishment.

"Didn't you hear?" the widow Thoms exclaimed. "Sherlock Holmes just asked me to marry him."

CHAPTER NINE

I rarely saw Sherlock Holmes that last week before the opening day of the Trans-Mississippi Exposition. A brief chat over breakfast was our only chance for communication. As stated before, he worked at the Exposition from eleven at night 'till seven in the morning. Then, after breakfast, he would don the uniform of an army lieutenant, make some changes in his hair and facial features, and report to Captain Lewellen's office downtown. It seems that the Captain asked Sherlock Holmes to do the final screening of applicants for the Expositions's private police force. Lewellen's appreciation for Holmes' ability overcame any military ego he might have possessed, which speaks very highly, in my humble opinion, for this man's overall leadership quality. As Lieutenant Holmes, in five short days he selected one hundred men from the thousands of applicants. You may be sure that loyalty to Holmes was the chief criterion for being chosen. Captain Lewellen was the official head of the Exposition police, but by opening day, Sherlock Holmes commanded his own private army of one hundred loyal troops.

During one of these breakfasts, while the widow Thoms was serving us our usual bacon and eggs, she suddenly braced herself for a moment, and then said, "By the way, Mr. Holmes, my answer is 'yes'."

To my astonishment, Holmes idly replied, "Of course, it is. I say, Watson, could you please pass the salt cellar?"

As Mrs. Thoms rushed happily from the room, I flushed beet red, and said, "See here, Holmes — I don't believe you realize what she just said 'yes' to."

"My dear Watson," he replied. "I am of necessity obliged to dwell in this abode. I realized from the instant of our arrival, that if I were to survive, I must shut that prattling female from my mind."

"But you don't understand —"

"Just as a wireless, in order to hear one frequency, shuts out all others," he went on, "I have perfected the ability to shut out just one frequency, so that I may hear all others."

"This is a bit more complicated," I protested.

"Watson, my friend, I do not wish to have to blot your voice out as well," he said with finality. "We will not discuss the widow Thoms again."

It was no small wonder that I was having such difficulty selecting a topic for my speech, living with two people who were so totally unaware of the other's intentions.

The opening day for the Exposition duly arrived. And I must own that it was truly spectacular. June 1st, 1898, in Omaha, Nebraska, was a day to be remembered. The parade started downtown, and continued to the Exposition grounds some four miles north. Since the parade was to pass Thoms' boarding house, I chose a comfortable chair on the front porch, and let the procession come to me. Mrs. Thoms and her three giggling daughters joined me, as the distant sounds of marching bands gradually became more distinct.

The first contingent to round the corner and come into our view was a troop of mounted Omaha policemen. Right behind them, also mounted on fine horses, were sixty smartly uniformed Exposition policemen, led by Captain Lewellen and Lieutenant Sherlock Holmes. Holmes saluted me smartly as he passed by, a salute which I proudly returned.

"Mr. Holmes must have been an officer in the army at one time," Mrs. Thoms observed. "He sits so straight on his horse."

"I'm afraid not," I replied. "But as you have probably noted, he plays many roles admirably."

"I've been wondering how my darling daughters should address him after we're married," she went on. "'Mr. Holmes' seems to be awfully formal. Yet, 'Sherlock' seems much too familiar coming from such little ones. Does he perhaps possess a nickname of some sort?"

"I suggest that you have them begin calling him 'Daddy' instantly. Perhaps that would locate an appropriate wave-length that would settle this thing once and for all."

John Phillip Sousa's famed United States Marine Band mercifully drowned out Mrs. Thoms'

attempts to further the topic. It was without question the finest band I have ever heard. It struck me as
very strange that this morning's headlines had
announced the first invasion of Cuba by four
hundred marines, while their official band was
marching toward a make-believe extravaganza out
here on the prairie.

The only other musical groups were local high
school bands, since all military and militia had been
called up to active duty. Only a force of two hundred
men remained at nearby Fort Crook. Most had been
shipped to a camp in the State of Georgia, prepara-
tory to the Invasion of Cuba. There was no doubt
now that the War with Spain was being fought more
hotly with each passing day. I could only wonder
how these events were going to reach out their
vicious tentacles to influence the Trans-Mississippi
Exposition.

Holmes assured me later that I would not have
enjoyed the crush of opening day at the Exposition
grounds. Besides the pushing crowds, many of the
exhibits were not yet complete. President McKinley
had addressed the throng by telephone, and pressed
a button in Washington that in turn started the
Exposition machinery.

"I was able to have a private telephone conversation with the President," Holmes said over breakfast the next morning. "He is indeed planning to
visit the Exposition, although he can't say when,
thanks to the war," Holmes went on. "By the way,
he thanks us for our help. And he asked me to pass
on his best personal regards to you."

"Well," I choked. "Indeed, I'm flattered." I
must confess that the President's remark was the
impetus that set me to work preparing speeches on

four different topics of medicine. I would give my colleagues at the Homeopath Convention their choice.

Actually, I threatened to prepare a fifth topic one day when the widow Thoms was being particularly talkative. For fifteen minutes running, she described the flower-girl dresses she was making to be worn by her daughters at the wedding. Seeing that I continued to write my paper in spite of her non-stop chatter, she finally inquired as to my topic.

"I am," I said emphatically, "preparing a paper on the ill effects of a disease that begins with a tensing of the diaphram, thereby producing a rush of air toward the larynx, the tautness of which is modified by the thyroarytenoids and other muscles, then pushed into the oral and sinus cavities before being expelled through the maxillary and mandibular labia."

"I don't believe that I've heard of that ailment," the widow Thoms said with complete bewilderment."

"I dare say," I said, "that your late husband was a victim of the disease."

"You're quite mistaken," Mrs. Thoms corrected me. "My John died of a heart attack."

"The heart attack was merely a symptom, my dear lady," I retorted. "I assure you that the chief cause of your deceased spouse's demise was that he was talked to death."

As practical head of the Exposition police, Lieutenant Holmes spent much of the next two weeks on the grounds, instructing his force on the finer points of security. To his credit, with one exception, no World's Fair ever had fewer serious criminal incidents.

For myself, I spent a great many afternoons as an ordinary visitor at the Exposition. My journal entries, letters to Mary, and work on my speeches were usually completed by noon. I would then take a brisk walk to the Exposition grounds, and partake of a light lunch at one of its many eateries.

I found the Midway to be most offensive. The noise was positively maddening, what with Wild West shows, barkers, sideshows, and musical extravaganzas. A major attraction was called "The Streets of Cairo", where people actually paid money to ride on camels. And the mechanical rides appeared to be positively life-threatening, including a "Giant See-Saw" that took carloads of people two hundred feet in the air — a huge barrel that sent people hurtling down a steep incline — and boats that shot down a man-made river at speeds of more than a hundred miles per hour. My skin turned clammy just watching such spectacles. I was certain that should I ever attempt to participate in such insanity, the result would be a state of apoplexy.

On the other hand, I thoroughly enjoyed the large exhibit buildings on the lagoon. The Electricity building was filled with spectacular displays of this most amazing energy form. The Government building documented the history of this young nation from the Revolution to the current conflict with Spain. I pored for hours in each of the buildings, all of which were true museums of the first order.

At long last, June 19th, the opening day of the Homeopath Convention, arrived. It was indeed the largest of all of the nearly one hundred national conventions attracted to Omaha by the Trans-Mississippi Exposition. So many medical people were present, that I wondered who, if anyone, was treating the sick people across the nation. It was with great trepidation that I sat through Mayor Moores' welcoming speech. The convention members milled the floor and talked to each other throughout the welcome, which didn't seem to bother the Mayor, who undoubtedly delivered the same speech to some convention or other every day. I then listened as Dr. Farnham orated a highly complimentary introduction of their guest keynote speaker, one John H. Watson, M.D.

As I stood at the podium, looking out at the sea of learned faces, I felt somehow unworthy of my task. I began by saying, "Gentlemen, first permit me to bring greetings from a fellow English physician to whom I personally owe a great deal — one whose name, I am sure, is legend even in America. I refer, of course, to A. Conan Doyle, M.D.

"Who in the devil is he?" a somewhat inebriated voice from the crowd shouted out.

"Surely," I said aside to Dr. Farnham, "that rude fellow is in jest."

"I confess that I have never heard of Dr. Doyle either," Dr. Farnham shrugged. "Perhaps it would be best if your proceeded with your topic."

"Very well," I said, a bit miffed. "Fellow homeopaths, I have prepared papers on four different topics."

"Boo," a chorus of voices replied. Obviously, a great many of these fellows used the convention as an excuse to partake of substances that would not be tolerated in their home towns.

"I will deliver only one of them, however," I shouted over the confusion, "the one which you feel will be most beneficial to your practice of medicine." I then patiently listed the topics, although I was never quite certain that anyone was listening. "Now," I asked, "which topic interests you most?"

"Where is Sherlock Holmes?" a voice shouted.

"He is working on an important case in Paris," I lied. "But I assure you that he also sends his best personal regards."

"What is Sherlock Holmes really like?" another voice asked. Then the truth finally dawned on me. These fellows were not the least bit interested in my medical opinions, even if I possessed such information that would really end all of the ailments that some of their patent medicines professed to cure. I had been asked to keynote this august assembly only because they were interested in Sherlock Holmes.

For the next two hours, I spoke of our adventures, carefully omitting the current one, and of Sherlock Holmes' compelling personality. I am told that it was the most appreciated address of all the conventions that met in Omaha in this important year of 1898.

CHAPTER TEN

If Holmes was surprised that he was the chief topic of my address, he failed to indicate it. His only reaction was a slight grunt, followed by the terse admonition, "Time to get back to work, Watson."

"I wasn't aware that I was sloughing," I said, a bit insulted.

"Sorry, old fellow," Holmes apologized. "I was implying nothing of the sort. But now that all of the exhibit materials have been shipped in, it's time for us to move into the next phase of our operation." There was a knock at the Thoms front door. "That will be Captain Lewellen."

True to Holmes' word, Captain Lewellen was indeed admitted by the widow Thoms.

"Why, Captain Lewellen," she exclaimed. "You haven't been by in ages. Do come in. I'll bet you haven't heard of my most fortunate news —"

"Mrs. Thoms," I cut in quickly. "Holmes and I have a great deal to discuss with Captain Lewellen, and very little time in which to do it."

"Oh very well," she pouted, as she retreated to the kitchen. In some ways, I was beginning to get the better of her.

"What made you send for me?" the Captain asked.

"It's time to ferret out any rats that may have crept into the Exposition halls," Holmes said with great elan. "All of the exhibitors are at last present, as is their equipment. A great many are working in total secrecy, which is quite understandable in most cases. Keeping their exhibits secret until they are ready to let the public view them protects their ideas from theft and their equipment from sabotage."

"Then what is it that worries you?" I asked.

"As you know," Holmes explained, "as a result of my recent manual labors, I have total knowledge of all public areas, as well as many of the private areas, of both the grounds and the buildings. But I don't know them all, especially the materials that have arrived since I retired from the construction trades."

"We could have our private police inspect anything that you consider suspicious," the Captain suggested.

"There are too many exhibits to inspect," Holmes said. "Then, too, a systematic search would forewarn any real enemy, and perhaps be illegal as well, considering the touchiness of those who put together your Constitution."

"Then what do you propose to do?" I asked.

"As head of security, Captain," Holmes instructed, "I want you to send telegrams to the governors of each state sponsoring an exhibit. Each is to contain precisely the same message. 'Urgent that you wire me instantly the full name of the person in charge of your exhibit.'"

"That's it?" Captain Lewellen asked.

"That will quite do the job, I assure you," Holmes replied. "Now, in two or three days, when you have received all of your replies, Watson and I will join you at your office to open them."

"Seems quite peculiar, Holmes," the Captain shook his head, "But, of course, you can count on me to carry out your orders."

"Good," Holmes said. "Now, Captain, if you will be good enough to procure materials for me according to this list, and have our trusted guards deliver them to the old barn on the back of this property this afternoon, it would be greatly appreciated."

"The widow has agreed to this, I presume?" I asked.

"That is your responsibility, Watson," Holmes replied. "I notice that you seem to have established some sort of rapport with her."

"Rapport, indeed," I snorted.

Mrs. Thoms was more than willing to make the old barn available, once she learned that the request was on behalf of her betrothed. Later that afternoon, a wagon pulled up, and two of Holmes' Exposition guards unloaded the supplies as requested.

Next morning after breakfast, I retired to update my journal, and to write my usual letter to Mary. Holmes retired to the old barn behind the Thoms boarding house. Each of my sentences were punctuated not only with commas and periods, but with the sounds of hammering and sawing as well.

When my chores were complete, I ventured out to the barn. There I found Sherlock Homes fashioning what appeared to be a packing box, six feet long by about three feet wide and deep. One of the long sides was open.

"I see that your carpentry work at the Exposition has become an addiction," I observed. "If you ever decide to retire as a consulting detective, you will obviously never starve."

"Actually, I've had a talent with wood from an early age," Holmes said, never slowing in his work. "As teenagers, my brother, Mycroft, and myself once constructed a coffin that was absolutely air-tight.

"Holmes," I said in total shock. "Surely that thing that you're building is not a coffin?"

"Come, come, Watson," he scoffed. "Something this crude would hardly be appropriate. However, the one that Mycroft and I fashioned was ultimately used for that purpose, donated to an unfortunate but destitute acquaintance of our father."

"What in the world possessed you to build a coffin?" I asked, with an involuntary shudder.

"An air-tight coffin," Holmes corrected me. "I wanted to experiment with ways of dropping my respiration rate to a level that would permit me to stay alive for long periods of time under such conditions. How could I perform such experimentation without a laboratory?"

"Considering my own fear of confined spaces, such a thought makes my flesh crawl," I said.

"Mycroft's reaction was much the same, I fear," Holmes sighed. "I reached the point where I could last two full hours, which I have no doubt one day will save my life. Poor Mycroft was in a frenzy within thirty seconds of the lid closing. If you consider his excessive weight, it's not surprising that he had so little control over other bodily functions." I suppressed an urge to remind Holmes of his own addiction.

Finally, Holmes completed the open-sided box to his satisfaction, and immediately began constructing a panel that would indeed enclose the open side of the box. He attached hooks to the four corners of the panel, and corresponding "eyes" on the inside corners of the open side of his box. He then stood the box on end.

"Watch this, old fellow," he said. He picked up the panel, and began backing into the open box.

"Let me give you a hand," I offered.

"If this is to be successful," he replied, "I must be able to perform it absolutely unaided." He backed slowly into the box, holding the panel only by its top two hooks. I could hear them snap into place in their appropriate interior "eyes". Holmes then put his thin body into a squat, and I could hear the two lower hooks snap into place as well. "Now," Holmes' hollow sounding voice resounded from the chamber, "examine the box and see if you can detect that perchance someone might be hiding inside."

"Of course, I can't," I said. "There isn't a trace of evidence to that effect."

"Splendid," Holmes said, as he quickly unfastened his hooks, and emerged from the box. "Now all we have to do is wait for the replies to our telegrams."

Holmes was not precisely true to his words, as he worked in his room with some chemical concoctions well into the night. At about four o'clock in the morning, I awakened briefly as I heard Holmes shout, "That did it!" I wondered briefly what it was he had done, and then slipped back into the arms of Orpheus.

The next evening, Holmes and I were chatting amiably over our dinner, when the widow Thoms, which was not her custom, joined us at the supper table.

"I dislike interrupting," she said, "but Mr. Holmes, there are certain details which simply must be discussed..." She was interrupted herself by a loud knocking at the front door.

"I am quite certain that you, dear lady, are thoroughly capable of anything requiring details," Holmes said. "Now, would you please admit Captain Lewellen's emissary to these premises, and show him back to us."

As Holmes predicted, our visitor was indeed the Captain's aide, who handed Holmes a note, which he quickly read.

"Make short work of your roast beef, Watson," Holmes announced. "The Captain has received the replies to our wires."

Lewellen's aide drove us quickly to the Captain's headquarters, which had now been relocated at the Exposition grounds in the Fire and Police building located on the lagoon. A pile of unopened telegrams covered the Captain's desk.

"Let us begin," Holmes said with great anticipation. "Here, Watson, is the master list of directors of each of the State buildings, which was supplied by the Exposition commissioners. Captain Lewellen and I will read the names supplied by the state governors in their telegrams, and you will see if they agree."

The tedious process began. The first twenty or so were in total agreement. On more than one occasion, the Captain and I exchanged puzzled glances, wondering perhaps if Holmes' great mind had finally collapsed under the strain. The telegram from the governor of Oregon, however, had a name that was at odds with the one on my master list.

"Is that what we've been looking for?" I asked in bewilderment.

"I doubt it," Holmes replied. "But we will want to have an explanation in any case. Let's carry on."

Only three telegrams remained unopened, when Lewellen unfolded the one from the governor of Louisiana. "Now here's a strange one," he said. "What do you make of this? 'My dear Captain Lewellen: There must be some misunderstanding on your part. Louisiana has no exhibit at the Trans-Mississippi Exposition. Yours truly, et cetera.'"

"That's it!" Holmes shouted as he leaped to his feet in triumph. "Gentlemen, we have struck the mother lode."

Holmes called in his corps of sergeants, as Captain Lewellen dispatched his aide to check on the Oregon discrepancy. He asked them what knowledge they had of the Louisiana exhibit and the people who worked on it. It was quickly established that they possessed very little information, except that their building exterior appeared to be complete. The exhibit itself was not yet open, and all interior work was being done in utmost secrecy, which was fairly common among the exhibitors.

Like so many of the other small State buildings, it was windowless and had only one means of exit and egress. That door was opened only when someone was entering or leaving. At ten o'clock each night, as the Exposition was closing for the night, the workmen would bar and triple-lock the door before leaving the Exposition grounds. The extent of the Louisiana building security seemed a bit extreme by other State building standards.

Their director was one Lesley Russell, a friendly enough chap, but who ran his construction and exhibit crews in a military manner. The workers themselves were very quiet, and kept exclusively to themselves. All Exposition business had to be conducted with Director Russell himself.

The discrepancy in the Oregon directorship proved, as Holmes had predicted, to be legitimate. The director mentioned in the telegram from the governor had died on the way to Omaha, and the Oregon delegation had simply designated his assistant as the exhibit director when they reported in to the Exposition.

For a week, Holmes himself, in a variety of disguises, shadowed the mysterious Lesley Russell, until he ultimately saw Russell board a train for Kansas City.

"We must move quickly," Holmes said, as he summoned Captain Lewellen, myself, and two sergeants to the old barn behind the Thoms boarding house. He carefully filled out two official shipping labels, pocketing one, and pasting the other on the strange box that he had constructed earlier. Other labels, saying "Extremely Fragile", "Handle with Care", and "This Side Up" were also attached to the crate. Holmes then put an envelope filled with some strange chemicals into his coat pocket. He then backed into the box, as he had previously demonstrated, and fastened the hooks.

"If we hurry," Holmes voice echoed from

within, "the sergeants can deliver this crate to the Louisiana building just before the Exposition closes for the night."

Lewellen and I held on tightly to the box, as the two sergeants prodded the horses that pulled our carriage through the darkness toward the Exposition grounds. The nightly fireworks spectacular that signalled the close of the Exposition grounds for the night lit up the sky in front of us. As the two sergeants loaded Holmes' box on a dory of sorts, Captain Lewellen and I hurried to our hidden observation post in the structure opposite the entrance to the Louisiana building. Just as we settled into our hidden observatory, we witnessed the two sergeants delivering their secret human cargo. When they were about twenty feet from the doorway, two particularly burly fellows appeared, and blocked their way. From our distance, Captain Lewellen and I were unable to hear their conversation. But Sherlock Holmes, who was of course quite nearby, reported that it went as follows.

"Where do you think you're going?" one of the large chaps demanded to know.

"We have a delivery for a Mr. Lesley Russell," one of the sergeants replied. "The shipping label says that he is to open it personally."

"Mr. Russell is out of town until Thursday afternoon," the other giant said. "So you'll have to take it back to the warehouse until then."

"Sure," the second sergeant said. "We'll do it first thing in the morning — unless one of you would like to sign for it."

"We can't sign for anything," the first man said. "Only Mr. Russell can accept shipments."

"That's fine with us," the second sergeant said agreeably. "We'll just let it sit here till tomorrow morning. You won't have to worry about its contents, by the way, because we have security police posted throughout the Exposition grounds all night."

"And speaking of security," the first sergeant said, "you had better get your building locked up for the night. The grounds must be cleared of unauthorized personnel in less than five minutes from now." The sergeants quickly took their leave, and left the two burly chaps in a quandary.

"What will we do?" Sherlock Holmes heard the one fellow ask, from his vantage point in the box.

"I don't know," his cohort replied. "If this box contains what I think it does, we don't dare leave it out here where some curious guard might decide to inspect it."

"On the other hand," the first man said, "the colonel told us not to accept any merchandise unless he authorized it."

"If we open it," the other man said, "we might just as well ask permission to face a firing squad."

After considering the situation for a moment, the first man exclaimed, "I've got it! Let's put the box in the building for safe-keeping overnight. And then, even though we're not on the day shift, we'll come in early, move the box back out, and guard it until the security policemen come and take it back to the warehouse." I could see his companion nod his agreement, and they carefully carried Holmes' box into the Louisiana building.

"So far, so good," I observed, heaving a sigh of relief.

"Keep your revolver ready in any case," Captain Lewellen cautioned. "I won't be content until those men emerge from the building."

"I shan't be content until Sherlock Holmes emerges from that building tomorrow morning," I replied.

At that point, the two burly fellows came out, quickly barred and triplelocked the door, and exited as the loudspeaker blared, "The Trans-Mississippi Exposition grounds are now closed for the night. All visitors and exhibitors must clear the buildings and grounds immediately."

Within a few minutes, the spectacular exterior lighting effects were shut down one by one, the constant din of voices and machinery were hushed, and Captain Lewellen and I settled down to a night of eerie silence, broken only occasionally by the footsteps of a passing security policeman.

Captain Lewellen snored quietly on the couch, as I took the first three-hour watch. Our task was that of a safety valve for Holmes. Should someone decide to penetrate the security police, and attempt to enter the building, we would rush them, firing our guns into the air. The security police would thus be alerted, and could legitimately take the culprits into custody, regardless of who they might be, for being on the grounds during unauthorized hours. The intruders would be held until Holmes was safely out of the Louisiana building, thus preserving the secrecy of our espionage. The only flaw in such a plan would be if either myself or the Captain fell asleep at our watch, an event we were determined would never occur.

I reasoned that I could help myself to stay awake by memorizing every detail of the Louisiana building exterior. Like virtually all of the more than one hundred buildings constructed for the Exposi-

tion, it was an ivory white in color. The relatively
plain wooden construction had been high-lighted
with tasteful light blue shading. Plaster of Paris
cornices graced each of the four corners of the flat
roof. A triangular facade jutted out from the front,
supported by four doric columns. Each column had
a larger-than-life piece of statuary set in back of it
near the front wall of the building.

As my mind wandered from the building exterior, I couldn't help but wonder the nature of
Holmes' adventures behind those sealed doors
across the way. What secrets did the Louisiana
building hold? Did they present a threat against
President McKinley during his proposed visit?

Then my imagination began playing cruel
tricks on me. Holmes would have no trouble getting
out of the crate, that was certain. But what if he were
unable to re-secure himself back in the box when his
spy mission was complete? True, he had already
performed the task twice. But never in the dark.
True, he had a lantern with him; but what if it failed
before his re-entry were completed? Or what if he
had an equipment failure? Open discovery in the
morning by the two frightened giants would surely
result in his murder.

"Blast it, Watson," I muttered aloud to myself.
"This is Sherlock Holmes you are talking about, not
some rank amateur."

"What's that?" Captain Lewellen asked grogg-
ily from the couch.

"Sorry, old fellow," I whispered. "It shan't
happen again."

I am happy to say that the night passed without
event. The gates were opened early for exhibitors
and workmen. Within seconds of the opening, the

two burly chaps from the night before rushed up to the door of the Louisiana building, looking as if their very lives depended on it. One kept a furtive watch, as the other hastily opened the locks on the door. The bar was raised, the door opened, and in an instant they were inside with the door closed. I held my breath as the fears of equipment failure re-invaded my imagination. It struck me that the men were gone much too long. As I released the safety on my revolver, the door to the Louisiana building opened, and the two men carried Holmes' crate to its previous location outside.

"We made it," one of the men sighed. "Thank the gods that we were the first ones here." The other man quickly relocked the building, as our faithful sergeants returned with their dory.

"See," the one sergeant said. "I told you that your merchandise would be safe out here."

"Yes, you were certainly right," one fellow replied. "Mr. Russell will return tomorrow afternoon, and I'm sure that he will be happy to claim this crate then at the warehouse."

As they started to load it on the dory, one of the sergeants exclaimed, "I'm afraid that we almost made a dreadful mistake. The shipping label says that this crate should have been delivered to the 'Indiana' building, not the 'Louisiana' building."

"But I saw it myself," one of the husky men said with disbelief. "It distinctly said that it was to be opened by Mr. Lesley Russell personally."

"See for yourself," the other sergeant said. "The shipping label says that it's to be opened personally by Mr. Russell Letsky of the Indiana delegation."

"We're certainly sorry for our mistake," the first sergeant said. "Obviously, yesterday was an extremely difficult and tiring day for all of us."

"We must rush this over to Mr. Letsky at the Indiana building," the second sergeant said. "Thank goodness no harm was done. But just to make sure that you fellows don't get into any trouble with Mr. Russell, we will be happy to stop by when he returns tomorrow afternoon, and explain the entire matter to him." The two men exchanged glances that bordered on terror.

"That won't be necessary," one of them said. "We will explain it to him ourselves."

"What's going on here?" a man who was obviously the leader of the day crew asked, as he approached the scene. "What are you two men doing here? You're on the night crew."

"We decided to see the rest of the Exposition today," one of them said quickly.

"That's right," the other quickly confirmed. "But we decided to stop by here first. And these sergeants were here mistakenly trying to deliver this crate to the Louisiana building instead of the Indiana building. Isn't that correct, sergeant?"

"Indeed it is," the sergeant said. "These men should be commended for their alertness, as well as their honesty. It would have been tragic if they had accepted it, and deprived the State of Indiana of its rightful property."

So saying, Holmes' crate was wheeled safely toward the Indiana building, where Captain Lewellen and myself rushed to join him.

CHAPTER ELEVEN

Since the sergeants had the burden of transporting Holmes in his crate without injuring him, Captain Lewellen and I managed to reach the Indiana building in advance of their arrival. The Indiana delegation had been most cooperative the previous day, once "Lieutenant" Holmes had explained the possible gravity of the situation. In the event that the two burly fellows were to follow the sergeants, they would discover that a "Russell Letsky" was indeed an official, though mythical, high ranking member of the Indiana delegation.

The crate was duly delivered, and moments later, "Lieutenant" Holmes emerged from it, looking refreshed and rejuvenated.

"Great work, all of you," Holmes congratulated us. "It was a most fascinating night. Gentlemen, we have stumbled on to an incredibly dangerous situation." Holmes then gave us the following account of his discoveries in the Louisiana building. "After our two accommodating friends moved my crate into the building, they briefly considered opening it, but then thought better of it," Holmes began. "And no small wonder, I was soon to learn. After their departure, I quickly let myself out of the crate, and lit my lamp. Since the building has no windows, there was no danger of the lamp being seen from the outside."

"Quite true," I concurred. "The Captain and I were scarcely fifty feet from the door, and I could detect nothing."

"My first discovery, however," Holmes continued, "could well have done me in, had I let my lamp come in contact with it. The Louisiana building contains no exhibits, but it does contain three bombs comprised of a large amount of explosives."

"Great heavens!" I exclaimed.

"What in the world do they propose to do with such a large quantity of explosives?" the Captain queried.

"Level the entire Trans-Mississippi Exposition," Holmes replied calmly. "In one series of massive blasts."

"I'll organize my men," Captain Lewellen announced, "and we'll storm the Louisiana building as soon as possible. Sergeant, call in all shifts to report to the Fire and Police building as soon as possible."

"I don't think that would be wise, Captain," Holmes cautioned him.

"Well," the Captain said with barely concealed indignation. "What would you suggest that we do?"

"For the moment," Holmes said, "nothing."

"You can't be serious, Holmes," I said in disbelief. "Literally thousands of innocent lives are being risked every day the Exposition opens."

"I agree that there is a certain element of risk in waiting, gentlemen," Holmes replied, but I believe that you will agree with me once I have explained everything. It took me almost two hours to solve the combination on the large safe, but it was well worth the trouble. The leader of the so-called Louisiana delegation, Mr. Lesley Russell, is quite another person indeed. I might add that he keeps a fascinating journal that would rival Dr. Watson's for its detail."

"For heavens sake, Holmes," I exclaimed, "if Lesley Russell isn't Lesley Russell, who in the devil is he?"

"Devil, indeed," Holmes mused. "An excellent choice of words, Watson. Our friend Lesley Russell is in reality one Matthew Huston, a most nefarious fellow, who is also known as 'The Chameleon', thanks to his ability to vanish every time the authorities think they have him trapped. He is an amazingly talented man, with great athletic and gymnastic abilities. Despite his age of almost forty years, he is capable of great feats of climbing and leaping."

"I've never heard of him," I said, somewhat dismayed.

"Nor I," Captain Lewellen added.

"As I stated earlier," Holmes explained patiently, "I keep a mental list of most of the more notorious criminals in the world. Matthew Huston in the leader of a small but vicious gang supposedly devoted to restoring the South to nationhood."

"What is he, then?" I queried. "Patriot or criminal?"

"A little of each, I surmise," Holmes said.

"Although Southern leaders officially despise Huston and his activities, a few wealthy zealots still believe that he might be the difference in establishing a new Confederate nation. His most detailed journal, however, indicates that he successfully collected four different fees for his Trans-Mississippi caper, so the greed motive can hardly be discounted entirely."

"But where does he come from?" Captain Lewellen asked.

"And what does he hope to accomplish?" I added. "Surely he is no threat to President McKinley."

"Initially that was part of the plan," Holmes said. "But the War with Spain has delayed the President's visit so long — plus the fact that the war is going so well for America — another approach had to be taken. I suspect that our Mr. Huston, alias Russell, is currently visiting in Kansas City with some of his benefactors on this matter right now. In answer to your question, Captain, it seems that Mr. Huston's father was killed at the Battle of Gettysburg during the Civil War. Huston was a young lad at the time. And since his father had been little more than a small-time hoodlum, it isn't surprising that he followed in his father's footsteps. Through the years, he has run his small army in a particularly brutal fashion, leaving few witnesses to his many crimes. On more than one occasion, some far less grave than the one that permitted my entry to the Louisiana building, he has had his own men summarily executed by firing squad. Small wonder those poor devils were in such a quandary over my packing crate. Yet, due to his supposedly patriotic cause, he has had little difficulty in recruiting replacements."

"But what does he hope to accomplish by merely blowing up the Exposition?" I asked, "and undoubtedly taking hundreds of innocent lives?"

"The safe in the Louisiana building contained many damaging documents," Holmes explained, "all of which are most certainly forgeries, linking the destruction with a supposed conspiracy of the entire former Confederacy leadership. It is his hope that by leaving these documents behind, this will spur a new conflict between North and South. Except that this time, the North will be fighting an all-out war with Spain as well. With wars on two fronts, these Southern patriots believe that the North will agree to separation as part of an overall peace settlement. Since it appears that President McKinley is delaying his visit to the Exposition until after the successful conclusion of the conflict with Spain, Mr. Huston will be forced to move earlier if the destruction of the Exposition is to be of any benefit to a new South."

"You know," I mused, "it just might have worked."

"All the more reason to strike at the Louisiana building at once," Captain Lewellen said, banging his fists together.

"Not so," Holmes admonished him. "I have copied Colonel Huston's map of the Exposition. I have marked the carefully concealed locations of each explosive device. From the looks of things, I would estimate that they will plant the remaining bombs tomorrow, just as they have been planting bombs all along during low attendance days. My examination of the explosives in the Louisiana building indicates that they are equipped with timing devices which will provide these fellows with up to three hours to make their escape."

"So?" I asked.

"So this is no suicide mission," Holmes replied. "We know that their leader, Matthew Huston, will return from Kansas City on Thursday."

"That's tomorrow," Captain Lewellen observed.

"Correct," Holmes said. "And I am certain that he will return with a new set of instructions. I am equally certain that they will attempt to carry out their plan within the day."

"Aren't we playing this thing awfully close?" I asked. "Perhaps the Captain is correct." I should have been wiser than to contradict Sherlock Holmes in any way, save there were so many lives at stake.

"I assure you, my dear Watson," Holmes' patience was obviously strained to the limit, "there will be infinitely less danger in waiting than there would be in making a cavalry charge on the Louisiana building. Now, Captain," he seemed to be dismissing me, "I have a plan. I distinctly recall having hired five of our Exposition guards who had experience with handling of munitions. Have them waiting at your headquarters when the Exposition closes for the night. Watson, my friend, I of course want you here as well. We will discuss the details then. Right now, I will require a few hours of rest, as I shall not be sleeping much for the next twenty-four hours. The cot at our clandestine viewpoint opposite the Louisiana building shall suffice. I should like to be awakened at about four this afternoon, after which time the three of us shall map our strategy. Meanwhile, have your men patrol the Exposition as usual. We don't want these fellows to suspect that we have caught up with them."

CHAPTER TWELVE

True to his word, Holmes fell fast asleep in a matter of minutes. He had indeed experienced a busy night in the confines of the Louisiana building. As observed earlier, it had taken him a full two hours to solve the combination on the safe. He spent the next several hours copying most of the documents it contained. And it had taken him another hour to reset the five traps that Colonel Huston had set to determine if anyone had tampered with his safe or document. The "Chameleon" was both clever and thorough. But he had never met the likes of Sherlock Holmes.

For myself, I felt no need for sleep. I had managed almost five hours of slumber during Lewellen's watches the previous night. And the sheer horror of realizing that a number of time-bombs were in place around the Exposition made sleep there a total impossibility.

So I determined to return to the widow Thoms' boarding house for a late breakfast, after which I would update my journal and write a letter to my dear Mary. Captain Lewellen was kind enough to transport me on his way to a meeting with the Mayor downtown. Per Holmes instructions, we agreed to confide our recently acquired information to no one.

As I entered the front door, the widow Thoms let out a small shriek as she leaped to her feet, attempting to shield something from my view.

"Dr. Watson!" she exclaimed nervously. "Is — is Sherlock Holmes with you?"

"As a matter of fact, no," I replied.

"Thank goodness," she sighed, with obvious relief. "It would have been the worst of bad luck."

"What in the world are you hiding?" I demanded to know.

"The material for my wedding gown arrived just today," she said, stepping to one side. "I know that it's unlucky for the groom to see his bride's gown before the wedding. So I presume that the same would hold true for the material. Would you by any chance know for certain, Dr. Watson?"

"I haven't the faintest idea," I sighed. "But I really wish that you would discuss this with Holmes before you incur any additional expenditures."

"Dr. Watson," the widow censured me, "I do believe that you are jealous of your friend's new-found happiness." So saying, she carried the package of white material to her own quarters.

I had scarcely completed my journal entries and epistle to Mary, when the Captain called for me with his carriage. As the horses clattered their way toward the Exposition grounds, I could not help but wonder what adventures awaited us over the next twenty-four hours.

Captain Lewellen and I slipped into the structure opposite the Louisiana building just as Holmes was arising. My pocket watch confirmed that it was almost four o'clock in the afternoon.

"Ah," Holmes said. "Captain Lewellen and my dear friend, Watson, right on time."

"I confess," the Captain said, "that I don't recall one word that was uttered during the meeting with the Mayor today — even though the discussion was concerned with security for President McKinley's visit, should that ever come to pass."

"It will," Holmes said confidently. "But first, we must make certain that there is an Exposition for him to visit. Now, gentlemen, here is my plan for not only defusing the bombs, but for capturing the elusive 'Chameleon' as well."

For the next four hours, Holmes explained his maps and plans to us. The three of us dined late at the Chinese village, where Holmes proved his expertise with those infernal chopsticks.

Before the grounds closed, at ten o'clock, the usual fireworks display lit the sky above this enchanted village. I must confess that I fairly shuddered at the thought of all those exploding rockets flashing over the many bombs concealed throughout the Exposition grounds. Soon after, the grounds were closed for the night, and the three of us joined Holmes' hand-picked police force at the Fire and Police building on the lagoon.

"I am certain," Holmes said, after everyone was present, "that Hustons's men suspect nothing at this time. But we must not under-estimate the 'Chameleon' himself when he returns tomorrow afternoon. Although he is almost forty years old, he is a superb athlete and acrobat. Mentally he is a genius, with a special cunning for military matters. He has never been captured, and vows that he never will be. He seems to be able to perceive the best baited trap intuitively. So everything and everyone must appear as normal and routine as possible."

"What's to be our plan then?" I asked.

"During the night, we will locate every concealed bomb," Holmes replied, "using the map that I copied from Huston's safe last night. There are twenty-four of them in all."

"And then of course disarm them," Captain Lewellen said with gusto.

"Not tonight," Holmes said. "That would forewarn Huston's henchmen, and the 'Chameleon' would vanish before he ever got to the Exposition grounds. No, my dear Captain. We will lay a trap that will put an end to this devil and his gang of cut-throats as well."

"Pray continue, Holmes," I prodded.

"We will determine how best to disarm the bombs once Huston's men have set the timing devices," Holmes went on.

"This sounds much too dangerous," the Captain said, shaking his head.

"According to Huston's journal," Holmes continued with no small amount of irritability, "the deed will be perpetrated just after four o'clock tomorrow afternoon. The change in work shifts will place all twenty-four of his cohorts on the Exposition grounds at once. If all goes well, each man will set a timing device, then all return to the Louisiana building. The documents that blame the former South leadership for their cowardly act will be removed from the safe and placed where they can easily be found. They will then leave the Exposition grounds, go to a nearby stable where horses have been left for them, and be three hours away when the Trans-Mississippi Exposition is reduced to rubble."

"How do you propose to stop them?" I queried.

"Once they have all departed the grounds," Holmes replied, "our men will quickly render the bombs harmless. And a military contingent from nearby Fort Crook will be waiting for them at the stable. The area around the stable will of course be cleared of all civilians."

"Then Colonel Huston and his men will have their choice of fighting and being killed," I mused, "or surrendering and being hanged."

"It sounds too simple," Captain Lewellen remarked.

"Indeed it might not be," Holmes said. "According to the 'Chameleon's' journal, if they suspect that they have been detected, they will set the timing devices for a ten-minute detonation, and each leave the Exposition on his own as best he can. They will not go to the stable, but will rendezvous at a place in the South, code-named 'Blue Plantation'."

"How do you propose to prevent that?" I asked.

"Our entire force of one hundred Exposition guards will be on duty tomorrow afternoon," Holmes replied, "although most will be kept out of sight, so as not to alert Huston and his men. Each bomb will have three of our trusted guards posted nearby. After Huston's men set the timing device, should they fail to return to the Louisiana building, our guards will confront them instantly. They have orders to capture them if possible, or kill them if necessary. Obviously, this presents a greater danger to visitors than the first plan. But since we will have three of our guards subduing each of Huston's men, it should be accomplished without incident. If shooting breaks out on the Exposition grounds, yet another military group will seal all the gates and surround the entire area. But let us hope that the latter plan will not prove necessary."

During the next few hours, we toured the darkened Exposition buildings and grounds with the five guards who had knowledge of explosives. One by one, we located the concealed bombs, being careful not to disturb them. Our experts agreed that the devices could be disabled by cutting two small wires below the timing device, and agreed to teach this tactic to every member of the Exposition police force the following day.

Holmes rehearsed the men in methods for apprehending the individual miscreants with the least possible danger to Exposition visitors. They agreed to pass this information on to their fellow guards on the morrow as well.

We then settled down to a restless night of fitful sleep, as each of us contemplated the events of the next day.

CHAPTER THIRTEEN

A regular visitor to the Exposition could not have dreamed that this day would be any different than those that had preceded it. The usual workers at the exhibits and buildings, including the Louisiana building, arrived on schedule. The gates were opened, and the usual multitude of visitors began making the turnstyles ring.

By noon, every eating place on the Midway was crowded with people. The "World's Largest Soda Fountain" had its twelve hundred seats filled to capacity, with the black onyx fountain jutting upward from the center of this maddening throng.

Holmes and I dined on sandwiches provided by Captain Lewellen in the structure facing the Louisiana building entrance. As we ate, we watched Huston's men coming and going from the building's single entrance. To look at them, one would never guess the havoc that they planned to wreak before the day was over.

At three o'clock in the afternoon, however, the air seemed to fill with the same electricity that pervaded these grounds and buildings after dark. Lesley Russell, alias Colonel Huston, alias the "Chameleon", strode into view, chatted amiably for awhile with an Exposition guard who was making his usual three o'clock rounds, and then disappeared into the Louisiana building.

"Good grief!" I exclaimed. "Perhaps we should have pulled that guard off his route today."

"That would most certainly have triggered Huston's suspicions," Holmes replied. "No my dear Watson. Everything must appear as normal as possible, if we are to trap this army as a group later at the stable."

Promptly at four o'clock, the second crew of twelve men arrived at the Louisiana building.

"The drama is about to unfold," Holmes said. "Have your revolvers at the ready, gentlemen."

As all twenty-four of Huston's cut-throats chatted as if this were a casual changing of work shifts, a most unfortuitous event occurred. A group of United States soldiers who were scheduled to be shipped to the Phillipine Islands had decided to celebrate their last day of liberty at the great Trans-Mississippi Exposition. They had obviously partaken of far too much of the fine wine featured at the California exhibit. As luck would have it, one of these chaps decided to shoot a few ceremonial blasts into the air, just as they were passing the Louisiana building. The shots prompted the arrival of several of our armed Exposition policemen, who thought that something had gone awry with our plans to capture Huston and his men.

"Curse it," Holmes expostulated.

The Exposition police quickly recovered, chided the errant soldiers for their misbehavior, and happily confiscated their firearms for the safety of all concerned.

"Maybe they won't suspect anything," Captain Lewellen remarked hopefully. "After all, it would be perfectly natural for our police to come on the scene when shots are fired anywhere on the grounds."

"There were too many of our guards on the scene," Holmes said. "And they arrived much too quickly. You see? The 'Chameleon' and his men are acting in an extremely suspicious manner."

Indeed they were. All of Huston's men had crowded into the portico behind the pillars, as if to avoid being targets for the errant soldier's bullets. Moments later, they poured en masse into the Louisiana building, and the door closed.

"This is a bit of bad luck," Holmes said. "However, we should be able to take them at the bomb sites."

Presently the door to the Louisiana building opened, and one by one, its inhabitants strolled out, casually scattering to all corners of the Exposition grounds. I counted them as Captain Lewellen identified each of them. Ultimately, twenty-four men left the building — all except for the notorious Colonel Huston himself.

"What do you make of it, Holmes?" I asked, releasing the safety on my revolver.

"I'm not certain," Holmes replied. "On the face of it, it would appear that the 'Chameleon' is staying with his original plan."

"He waits behind," Captain Lewellen said, "while his men set the timing devices on the twenty-four bombs."

"When they return," I added, "they all leave the grounds and proceed toward our trap at the stables."

"Still and all," Holmes shook his head, "Huston had to be alerted by the presence of so many Exposition guards. However, we should know presently."

Holmes had no sooner uttered these words, when the sounds of shouting and shooting echoed throughout the grounds.

"Let's take Huston, now," Holmes commanded, as we rushed out of the building. Five Exposition policemen were charging through the door to the Louisiana building just as we arrived. The eight of us fairly tumbled into the building, revolvers readied for a showdown with this most despicable fellow.

"Great heavens," I shouted, "There is no one here!"

"Very astute, Watson," Holmes observed. "It would appear that our friend the 'Chameleon' has once again lived up to his pseudonym."

"But this isn't possible," Lewellen exclaimed.

"Surely there must be a secret exit," I said.

"I assure you that there isn't one," Holmes replied. "If you recall, I spent several hours in this building just a few nights ago. I went over every square inch of the walls and floors with my glass, and there is only one means of entrance and exit." Holmes was examining the area under a very expensive looking desk, "Aha," he exclaimed. "At least we have one bit of good luck."

"Then how in the world did he get out?" I asked.

"Watson, you must go back to the elementaries," Holmes said, rushing through the door to the porch outside. "After you have eliminated all but one answer, then, that answer must be true, no matter how illogical it might seem. Since there is no way out of the building except this door — we must conclude that he never entered it in the first place,"

"Confound it, Holmes," I stammered, "I saw him enter it with his men."

"What you saw was a large group of men enter the building," Holmes corrected me. "Aha," he said. "Here is our solution," Around the base of one of the larger-than-life statues that graced the porch of the Louisiana building, a group of glowing footprints began to appear.

"What in the world?" I exclaimed.

"It's the chemical that I compounded in my room a few nights back," Holmes explained, as he quickly examined the statue with his glass. "Very unstable in nature. When it's disturbed, it begins to glow after a short time. And large enough amounts adhere to a surface for some time, depositing small amounts of it as a person walks. During my recent visit to the Louisiana building, I spread a good deal of it under that rather ornate desk, knowing that it had to be Colonel Huston's private property. When he arrived this afternoon, he obviously spent some time at his desk, accumulating large amounts on his boots."

"But — where is he now?" Captain Lewellen asked.

"Watson and I will be tracking him shortly," Holmes replied. "But I do know where he was when we stormed into the building."

"For heavens sake, Holmes," I declared, "where was he?"

"Inside this statue," Holmes replied. So saying, he located a secret switch, and the rear half of the statue swung open like a door. "When the Exposition police arrived to calm our boisterous soldiers, the 'Chameleon's' cohorts shielded our view while their leader deposited himself in this most ingenious hiding place. After we charged into the building, he simply let himself out and vanished into the crowds."

At that moment, one of Lewellen's lieutenants rushed on to the scene and saluted. "Sir," he said breathlessly, "we have successfully subdued all of Huston's men, seven killed and seventeen captured."

"And the explosive devices?" the Captain asked.

"All disarmed," he replied. "We have one guard slightly wounded, and no civilian casualties. The guard has been removed to the Exposition hospital."

"Excellent," Holmes exclaimed. "Come, Watson. It's time to go after the 'Chameleon'. Captain Lewellen, have your men at full alert. If Watson and I are successful at flushing Colonel Huston into the open, they could prove quite useful in his capture. Remind them that he is armed and decidedly dangerous."

"The military have already sealed all entrances from the outside," Captain Lewellen said, "and have the grounds completely surrounded."

"Excellent," Holmes said with enthusiasm. "We do not want to miss this most fortuitous opportunity to end the 'Chameleon's' singularly notorious career."

Holmes and I immediately began following the trail of glowing footprints. Armed security guards were everywhere, calming the visitors and re-establishing order.

"I fail to see how this chap has any chance of escaping." What with the army of men pitted against him," I puffed, struggling with my lame leg to keep up with Holmes' rapid pace.

"He has every chance of getting away," Holmes replied. "This is by no means either the first or the largest army to attempt to capture him."

Presently the trail led us into a building appropriately labelled "The Big Rock". From the outside, it appeared to be precisely that — a huge boulder some fifty feet high and a hundred feet wide. But when we stepped through the door, my eyes were met with an extravaganza of great proportion. A "dancing devil" was chasing several "imps of hell" through an artificial rain and lightening storm that sent sheets of water cascading into an artificial lake. The dance ended with a rain of fire some fifty feet high and a hundred feet wide, punctuated with appropriate music. The electric lights came on as the show ended, and I realized that Sherlock Holmes was not in sight. While I had been mesmerized by the "Devil's Dance", Holmes had obviously continued the chase. With great difficulty, I pushed my way through the exiting throng, still following the eerie glowing boot-prints on the floor. They led me to what appeared to be a backstage dressing room, where I found Holmes bending over the inert figure of a young man who was clad only in his underclothing.

"Great heavens," I exclaimed. "Is he dead?"

"Just badly stunned," Holmes replied. As if to confirm Holmes' diagnosis, the young man stirred and sat up, rubbing a large contusion on the back of his head. "Dr. Watson, please meet private Jackson, one of the Exposition security guards, who my guess has made the unfortunate mistake of trying to capture the 'Chameleon' single-handedly."

"I saw him come into the building," Private Jackson winced with pain. "There was no time to seek help, so I tried to surprise him in this dressing room."

"But Huston knew you were coming," Holmes said, "and you were the one who was surprised."

I glanced quickly around the room. Colonel Huston's clothing, including his telltale boots, were strewn everywhere. The unfortunate Private Jackson's blue Exposition police uniform was nowhere to be seen.

"Obviously," I observed, "the man has disguised himself as one of the Exposition police."

"Or so he would have us believe," Holmes replied. "My guess is that he realized the tracks he was leaving, and determined to use this event to send us in a false direction."

"How so?" I asked.

"Note how large Colonel Huston's boots are, compared to the diminutive size of Private Jackson's bare feet," Holmes said. "Our friend the 'Chameleon' could not possibly force his feet into Jackson's boots."

"But — but," Private Jackson stammered, "he was actually putting on my uniform when he clubbed me. I saw it with my eyes."

"But," Holmes replied, "your own eyes were quite closed when he divested himself of your uniform, and donned whatever garment was in that closet, which Dr. Watson will discover is quite empty."

"So it is," I said, following Holmes' direction. As I gazed at the empty closet in amazement, a voice from behind us boomed, "What are you doing in my dressing room?" My eyes nearly fell out of my head when I turned and saw Satan himself framing the doorway.

"My dear fellow," Holmes replied, "perhaps you could give us a description of the clothing that you left in this room, when you changed into your present costume?"

The man told us that he was a member of a gypsy tribe, and clothed himself accordingly, with a white blouse, black pantaloons, and a red sash around his waist.

"Do you have some similar attire that would be our sizes?" Holmes inquired.

CHAPTER FOURTEEN

Within minutes, Holmes and I were back out on the Exposition Midway, clad in costumes that would have been more appropriate to a bad opera. The Midway had already returned to its boisterous normality, with barkers touting the merits of various sideshows, vendors offering a variety of useless wares, and the incessant wild rides rolling and shooting down the bluff. This portion of the Exposition fairly drove me to madness, but the import of the moment made me bear up under such tasteless cacophony.

Holmes surveyed the scene for a few moments. I could tell that his great mind was attempting to penetrate the insidious brain of the "Chameleon".

Finally he said, "Watson, I have an important assignment for you."

"Anything," I said with obvious naivete, having no knowledge of the task at hand.

"You are aware of the description of the apparel that Colonel Huston is wearing," he said.

"Of course."

"I want you to ride to the top of the 'Giant See-Saw', and see if you can spot him from that vantage point," Holmes instructed.

"I would more happily take another bullet in my leg," I gasped. "Great heavens, Holmes, that contraption climbs two hundred feet in the air!"

"Precisely," Holmes said. "You should be able to scan the entire Exposition grounds. If you hurry, you can catch the next car. Pay especial attention to the rooftops, old fellow. Keep in mind that our man is a superb acrobat."

With great trepidation, I filed into the car with a gaggle of teen-aged females, who were obviously in a heightened state of anticipation over their impending journey into the clouds. As I sat down, the door to the cage was locked, and I felt myself and the car leave terra firma.

The machine was truly a "Giant See-Saw", with a cage at either end. While our car was being loaded at ground level, the cage at the other end hovered two hundred feet directly above us. As my cage rose into the air, the crossbar pivoted on the hundred-foot-high fulcrum, returning the other cage to Mother Earth as it bore myself and my chattering companions into the heavens. I gazed with terror at the descending cage opposite mine, wondering almost aloud if I would ever return safely from this insane mission that Holmes had concocted. I gasped as I realized that I was looking at none other than Colonel Huston in his gypsy garb, who was one of about a dozen passengers in the descending car.

"Holmes," I shouted from my rapidly rising cage. "Holmes, he is in the other cage." Holmes waved at me from the ground below, and ran toward the loading platform that the other cage was now rapidly approaching.

As I watched the car descend, I saw a hand reach through its safety bars, and spring the lock. Moments later, the "Chameleon" had climbed to the top of the cage, and leaped to the crossbar of the "Giant See-Saw". As the cage lowered, Colonel Huston ran up the crossbar toward the fulcrum. As it swung past a nearby building, he leaped a distance of about ten feet, just catching its cornice with one outstretched hand. Within seconds, he was on the roof, and racing for the next building.

Holmes ordered the operator to bring my car down directly. As I rapidly descended, I watched with amazement at the "Chameleon's" superb agility, till he disappeared over a rooftop in the "Streets of Cairo" section.

By the time I reached ground, Holmes had commandeered a military hack, and we raced for the spot where I had last seen Huston. When we reached the "Streets of Cairo" section, Holmes dispatched the hack with instructions for Captain Lewellen to seal the area.

We stood at the head of the "Street", and surveyed the situation. Shops and shows lined either side, and a large minaretted cabaret sealed off the other end. Camels lounged and roamed the "Street" more or less at will.

"I don't see how he can get away this time," I observed. "The street is a dead-end, and I know for a fact that there are no rear doors or windows to these buildings. When Lewellen gets here with his men, we will simply search each shop and sideshow until we find him."

"Don't underestimate this fellow, Watson," Holmes cautioned me. "He is incredibly inventive."

I scrutinized the entire street for some glimpse of Colonel Huston. But the only person in sight was a grubby looking Arab fellow, riding on a camel that seemed to be content to shuffle along at a slow pace. Suddenly the fellow kicked the camel violently, and it rushed straight for us in a wild gallop. My game leg didn't permit me the agility to move quickly enough, but fortunately Holmes plucked me from its path at the last possible instant. Animal and rider turned the corner and raced up the bluff.

"Quick, Watson," Holmes shouted. "We must press on."

So saying, he mounted a nearby kneeling camel, and kicked it into action. Without hesitation, I followed suit, and moments later was hurtling up the bluff on the largest, most foul-smelling beast with which I have ever come in contact. Huston had a good lead on Holmes, who was only a few yards ahead of me.

At the top of the bluff, Huston leaped from his mount, and raced to the loading platform for the "Rolling the Roll" amusement ride. He was threatening the young attendant with his pistol, as Holmes and I dismounted. As we, too, raced for the platform, Huston leaped into a barrel, and the frightened attendant pressed the button that sent him hurtling down the hill.

Holmes leaped into the next barrel, where I joined him, taking the seat opposite him.

"Quick, man," Holmes shouted at the attendant. "We must catch that dangerous criminal." The attendant quickly threw the switch, and Holmes and I were instantly hurtling down the bluff. I must confess that it was unlike any other sensation I had ever experienced. Holmes and I were sitting in a giant barrel that was rolling at juggernaut speed, yet our seats remained absolutely level. Had we possessed a table and chess set, we could have played without spilling any of the men. Seconds later, we rolled to a smooth stop, then continued the chase on foot.

The "Chameleon" was by now ascending the steps to a tall tower of another amusement ride entitled "Shooting the Chutes". Once again, Huston threatened the thoroughly frightened attendant, who quickly cut his boat loose on its journey down the bluff. And once again, Holmes and I gave chase. I could not believe that I had actually boarded this most dreaded of all attractions. Our boat raced at speeds of up to one-hundred-and-twenty miles per hour, as torrents of water cascaded past us in giant waterfalls. On four different occasions, our boat actually left the water and sailed out off the bluff, only to land gracefully back on the crashing stream, and continue its insane plummeting. Quite suddenly it came to a peaceful rest on a quiet artificial lake some three hundred feet below. It took exactly six-and-one-half seconds to make the journey, and we stepped out on the disembarking platform totally dry.

Our pursuit of the "Chameleon" was dreadful on my leg, but I managed to keep pace in spite of the pain. We chased Huston toward the lagoon area. By the time that we arrived, two petrified gondoliers were furiously poling Huston across the lagoon, toward the Government building at the far end. We procured the services of a gondola and crew, and continued the chase. Both Huston's and our craft threaded through the heavy lagoon traffic, dodging pleasure boats and other gondolas, as well as flocks of exotic waterfowl. We passed marvelous fountains and under quaint bridges that spanned the lagoon. By the time that we slid up to the other gondola and its two quaking crewmen, the "Chameleon" was climbing a beam to the top of the Government building, where he clambored up its golden dome and clung to the marvelous statue that had been mounted there, obviously surveying the scene outside the Exposition grounds.

"If he makes it down the other side of the Government building," I panted, "he will have escaped the Exposition grounds, and be away."

"That is precisely his plan," Holmes said. "But it will be to no avail."

Suddenly shots rang out from outside the Exposition, and several bullets ricocheted off of the great golden dome near Colonel Huston's feet. He quickly slid down the dome, and leaped to the top of an arcade that led to the buildings along the north edge of the lagoon. Racing along the top of the arcade and the buildings as well, he disappeared in the elaborate shrubbery that had been planted for this World's Fair.

"Let's be after him, Holmes," I shouted with a zeal that I had not felt since the Maiwand campaign. At that moment, Captain Lewellen arrived with a contingent of Exposition guards.

"We came as soon as we heard the shooting," the Captain said. "I take it that he got away again."

"I'm afraid so," Holmes replied.

"But by now he should know that he can't get off the Exposition grounds," I observed, "which means that he will eventually have to give himself up or be killed."

Holmes once again seemed to fall into a trance. After a few moments, he brightened up, and said, "Of course — there is one way out."

"Impossible!" I stated. 'The Exposition grounds are surrounded by two hundred military men sealing him in, and we have one hundred Exposition guards on the inside, seeking him out."

"Captain Lewellen," Holmes went on, "can I trouble you for the use of a hack and a driver. I need the fastest horses you possess."

"They are mine," Lewellen said, "and they are right here at your disposal."

"Excellent," Holmes replied. "Now, I would like to have you and your men delay the 'Chameleon' as long as possible. Set up checkpoints between here and the Bluff tract, searching and identifying everyone who goes through them."

"Do you think that will expose him?" the Captain asked.

"No," Holmes replied. "He will undoubtedly find ways through them or over them. But it should slow him down sufficiently that Watson and I can implement my plan."

"Then — you know where Huston is going?" Lewellen asked.

"We have no time to lose, Captain," Holmes said. "I shall explain it to you later."

Holmes and I boarded Lewellen's hack, and Holmes directed the driver to take the road along the south edge of the lagoon. The horses' hooves clopped steadily along the brick road. As we passed the many ornately festooned buildings, I reminisced about the events of the day.

"Why do you suppose that Huston went up on the 'Giant See-Saw?'" I asked. "After all, it did pose something of a trap."

"A trap for an ordinary person, perhaps," Holmes replied. "But Huston obviously planned his acrobatic escape in advance, should it prove necessary. As to his motives for going two hundred feet into the air, it was for purpose of reconnaissance. And you will note that he subsequently selected a path out of the Exposition grounds that was physically difficult, but totally unguarded. Had it not been for the military blockade of the grounds, he would have indeed made good his escape."

Holmes directed the driver up the hill, and had him pull up to the "California Gold Mining Tunnel" attraction near the edge of the bluff. We alit, and Holmes instructed the driver to get out of the vicinity as quickly as possible.

We approached the attendant, who was visiting with three young men clad in miner's outfits, complete with caps mounted with lanterns.

"Has anyone taken the tour recently?" Holmes asked.

"I'm afraid not," the attendant replied. "You're the first customers we've had in two hours."

"We are not customers. I am Lieutenant Holmes of the Exposition police. And you are about to help us capture a most dangerous criminal."

The three young men in miner's hats proved to be tour guides for the attraction. Their job was to accompany groups of visitors in a miner's basket that was lowered five hundred feet down a shaft to a replica of a California gold mine.

Holmes made a thorough inspection of the scene as well as the apparatus.

"Can the machinery be stopped and started during the basket's descent?' Holmes asked.

"Yes, it can," the attendant replied.

"Excellent," Holmes said. "Here is our plan. Two of you guides must loan Watson and me your hats. You three guides are to leave instantly, locate Captain Lewellen, and tell him to remove his checkpoints."

"But," I protested, "that will make matters easier for Huston."

"Precisely," Holmes replied, as the youths left the scene. "The quicker he gets here, the sooner it will all be over." Now, he turned his attention to the attendant. "I want you to lower Watson and me to the bottom of the shaft. Presently a lone man will approach you."

"What will he look like?" the young man asked.

"He is a master of disguise," Holmes replied, "so all I can be certain of is that he will be quite alone. He will point a revolver at you, and demand to be lowered to the bottom of the shaft."

"A re — revolver?" the lad choked. "A — loaded — revolver?"

"He shan't harm you," Holmes reassured him. "He needs you to operate the lift. Be certain to inform the man that once the machinery is started, it cannot be stopped until it has run full cycle to the bottom."

"But that isn't true," I corrected Holmes.

"Of course it isn't," Holmes replied. "When Huston's basket is about three hundred feet down the shaft, shut off the machinery."

"Brilliant," I said. "Huston will be trapped too far down to climb up the cable, and too far up to jump and survive."

"It will not be quite that simple," Holmes observed. "But it should mark the beginning of Colonel Huston's capture. Come, let us be on our way. You will of course not mention to Colonel Huston that we will be awaiting him at the bottom of the shaft."

As the cage was slowly lowered into the mine shaft, I was reminded once again of my feelings of claustrophobia. We turned up the lamps on our hats as the shaft darkened. About five feet from our cage was a grease-smeared cable which was going up the shaft as our cage was steadily lowering us five hundred feet to the "gold mine" below.

"Why in the world would the 'Chameleon' want to be lowered into this horrible hole in the ground?" I asked.

"Because it isn't a hole in the ground as such," Holmes replied. "During my pre-Exposition career as a carpenter, I actually helped construct it."

"It certainly looks like a mine shaft to me."

"Indeed it does," Holmes said. "But it is actually a shaft that goes down the side of the bluff, and is truly underground only the last twenty-five feet or so. As to why Huston will try this route, the answer is that there is an exit at the bottom. We must presume that a man as brilliant as Colonel Huston is aware of that fact."

"Why have an exit at the bottom of this shaft?" I asked.

"To service the Exposition water supply," Holmes informed me. "You see, part of this shaft is used to pump approximately one million gallons of

water every day from the adjacent Missouri River up
to the Exposition grounds."

It was a great relief when the basket in which
we were being transported came to a gentle rest on
firm ground. We left the cage, and it immediately
began grinding its way back up to the top of the
bluff. The greasy cable wound round a large pulley
that provided the leverage necessary to raise and
lower the cage.

Holmes immediately began exploring the "gold
mine". The proprietors of this most ingenious operation had taken advantage of the shaft that was
constructed to raise the water necessary to service
the many rivers, lakes and lagoons at the Exposition.
To complete the illusion of a California gold mine,
eight hundred feet of cross-cuts, drifts, veins and
ledges had been carved into the bluff, that created a
reproduction of a "California Gold Mine".

"Where is the location of this exit?" I enquired.

"There is a ladder at the beginning of this
tunnel." Holmes flashed his lantern toward it.

"It goes up to a trap door that opens to the
pumping station, which in turn opens onto the river
bank and freedom for Colonel Huston," Holmes
explained.

"But why aren't the military sealing off this exit
as well?" I asked.

"Because it isn't an official entrance to the
Exposition," Holmes replied. "And because it isn't
officially even on the Exposition grounds. Hello,
what's this? By jove, it's a tar barrel. Of course, such
material was needed to simulate the veining in the
side walls of our 'gold mine'."

"What's so unusual about that?" I asked.

"Nothing," Holmes replied. "But it could prove

useful. Help me to get the lid off." I found a steel bar and, in a matter of seconds, we had pried the lid off to discover that the barrel was nearly full of tar. "An excellent piece of good luck," Holmes beamed. "Help me to move it over by the large pulley." As if on cue, the great pulley began to move, as the cage above began to descend. "Quickly, Watson. Our trap is about to be sprung."

Holmes and I managed to half-slide and half-roll the barrel of tar into the position he wanted, just as the cable ground to a halt. "Aha! Everything is going as planned. Have your revolver ready."

"What can Huston possibly do but wait and be captured?" I asked.

"He undoubtedly commandeered the third miner's helmet for his trip down," Holmes said. "Right now, I would venture to say that he is shining his lantern on the cable, contemplating the five-foot leap from basket to cable. He recognizes that a bungled leap would result in a quick death. But he has no choice, because he has vowed never to be captured. He is now measuring with his eyes the amount of grease deposits on the cable, and wondering how rapidly his rate of descent will be even if he successfully catches on to the cable. He is wrapping his hands with part of his clothing, so as to better control his fall. Now he is making his leap for life —or death — or capture."

Moments later, a human figure came hurtling down the cable and crashed directly into the barrel of tar that Holmes and I had placed there. He was quite immobilized from the waist down.

"Colonel Huston, I presume?" Holmes said as amiably as if he had just received a formal introduction. "I figured that you would appreciate something to break your fall. Don't bother reaching for your revolver, by the way. It probably will not operate properly, what with the tar and all. And in any case, Dr. Watson has his revolver pointed directly at your right eye."

"Who in the devil are you?" Huston demanded to know. "No one one has ever managed to get this far out in front of me."

"I daresay, Colonel Huston," I observed, "that he has outwitted more evil geniuses than any man in the world."

"I must confess that you have proved interesting," Holmes admitted. "However, my dear 'Chameleon', I would venture to say that you will not be the most challenging adventure of the year 1898."

After Lewellen and his men were lowered into the "mine", Colonel Huston was loaded into the basket, complete with his tar barrel cocoon, and taken back up to the surface. He was formally arrested, and removed to the city jail, where he was chained and double-guarded while being held for Federal trial.

CHAPTER FIFTEEN

Later, Captain Lewellen was good enough to deposit me at the doorstep of the widow Thoms' boarding house, where it was my intention to get some badly needed rest. He and Holmes were to continue downtown in the Captain's carriage for a meeting with Mayor Moores.

With weary legs, I climbed the steps to the porch, and gratefully entered the premises. However, I was immediately set upon by the widow herself.

"Dr. Watson," she said gleefully. "Exactly the person I was hoping for. I hope that Sherlock Holmes is not with you."

"Your hopes are a reality," I observed. "And now, if you will excuse me, I should like to take to my bed."

"But I desperately need you for just a few minutes," she insisted. "Surely a brief favor for a landlady who has fed you so well isn't asking too much, is it?'

"Oh, very well," I conceded. After all, her point was well taken. "But only for a few minutes." Had I known what she had in mind, I would have returned to England forthright.

"I shall return momentarily," she shrilled, bustling toward the rear bedroom. True to her word, she re-entered the room shortly, carrying what was obviously a flowing white wedding gown.

"I'm to the point where I can continue no further," she explained, "until I hang it on someone to set the hemlines. And since you and I are very nearly the same height —"

"I daresay —" I spluttered. Before I could utter another word, the lacy gown was draped around my shoulders, and hanging clear to the floor.

"Up, upon this stool," she ordered, propelling me physically at the same time. Somehow the donning of that gown had rendered harmless whatever masculine resolve I could muster to refuse such an unseemly task. The next thing I knew, I was indeed standing docilely on the stool, whilst the widow busied herself with pinning the hem to its desired length.

"Oh, dear," she exclaimed. "I seem to have run out of pins. Oh, well. I have an extra package in my bedroom. Now, don't you move an inch, or you will ruin everything I've done, and we will have to start all over again."

With that unwholesome prospect firmly in mind, you may be assured that I did not move at all. Not even when Sherlock Holmes popped into the room to retrieve some papers that he had promised to deliver to Mayor Moores. Not even when Holmes remarked, "Watson, I fear that your career as a Master of Disguises is likely to be a short one." He was gone just before the re-emergence of the widow Thoms, pins in hand.

"I'm so glad that Sherlock Holmes did not return with you," she remarked. "You know, it's bad luck for the groom to see his bride's dress before the wedding."

"No worse luck, I assure,"I said, "than seeing his best friend modeling the blasted thing."

CHAPTER SIXTEEN

The summer of 1898 was destined to be long, hot and somewhat uneventful. The War with Spain was heating up even as the weather did. On June 25th, a brash young officer by the name of Theodore Roosevelt led his cavalry group called the "Rough Riders" into a hideous ambush that left thirteen of his men dead. He later did somewhat the same thing at a place called "San Juan Hill", and was for some reason or other declared an incredible hero.

However, the war generally was going well for our American hosts, both in the Caribbean Sea and on the Philippine Islands. It seemed only a matter of time before President McKinley would announce a date for his visit to the Trans-Mississippi Exposition.

For my part, I visited the Exposition grounds almost daily. It was my intent each day to study a new facet of one of the museums or art galleries and then perhaps take in a concert. But each day found me instead at the Midway, where I had become completely addicted to the wild rides and sideshows that I had previously so abhorred. Hardly a day passed that I didn't ride to the top of the "Giant See-Saw" or come rocketing down the bluff while "Shooting the Chutes". I rode the camels so routinely that they would trot right up to me when I called them by name. And I sincerely hoped that my saintly Mary would forgive my frequent trips to "The Streets of Cairo" to view the dancing girls. Of course, you must understand that it was purely because I was fascinated with the art form.

I received letters almost daily from my beloved Mary, who was beginning to wonder when I would be returning home to England. It seems that Mrs. Cecil Forrester's health was improving rapidly, and Mary would soon be returning home. I yearned to return to our quiet abode in London, but knew that I could not possibly enjoy its comforts until President McKinley safely completed his visit to Omaha.

CHAPTER SEVENTEEN

I was sitting in the parlor one Saturday morning in early July, reading the news that the United States had just annexed Hawaii. This interesting bit of news was interrupted when the widow Thoms entered, accompanied by a fellow who was clad in black.

"Dr. Watson," the widow addressed me, "I would like you to meet Father James Wickham. He is the rector of Grace Episcopal Church."

"Pleased, indeed," I said, rising and extending my hand.

"My pleasure, I assure you," Father Wickham replied. "I never dreamed that I would one day shake the hand of the famous Dr. Watson —"

"Why, thank you, I'm sure," I said with no small degree of pride.

"— let alone have the pleasure of uniting the

great Sherlock Holmes in holy matrimony with the good widow Thoms."

"I beg your pardon," I gasped, my jaw hanging open.

"Father Wickham was kind enough to help me set a wedding date," Mrs. Thoms said with a shy blush. "The first Saturday in September will be the day."

"No one is even supposed to know that Sherlock Holmes is in America," I sputtered, "with the exceptions of you, Captain Lewellen, the Mayor, and Chief of Police."

"I am a priest of the Episcopal Church," Father Wickham said with a huff. "Do you think that I would broadcast your secret to the world?"

"And just how do you propose to publish the banns?" I asked.

"I shall mumble them from the pulpit," Father Wickham said. "My parishioners accuse me of doing a great deal of mumbling. In any event no one shall understand his name, I assure you."

"And the wedding will be a private one," the widow explained. "Just my darling little ones, as flower girls, Captain Lewellen as a witness, and of course you will be Sherlock's best man."

"I must remember to hide his revolver," I muttered.

"Since Mr. Holmes is English," Father Wickham said, "the widow felt that he would be far more comfortable having the ceremony performed in an edifice that shared his Anglican heritage."

"Holmes would be more comfortable in the City jail, I daresay," I said. However, the Reverend Wickham seemed to be suffering from the same malady as the widow Thoms, with the capacity for being stone deaf to anyone's comments but his own.

Later in the day, I stopped in at the Fire and Police building at the Exposition. Holmes and Captain Lewellen were in a meeting which they invited me to join.

"Come in, my dear Watson," Holmes said cordially. "Captain Lewellen has just returned from a meeting with the Mayor and Police Chief regarding security plans for the President's visit."

"Then a date for the President's visit has been set?" I asked.

"No," Captain Lewellen said. "But it's fairly certain that he will come. If an announcement is not forthcoming soon, a delegation from Omaha will travel to Washington next month to coerce him."

"Meanwhile," Holmes said, "plans must be made for his security."

"Quite right," the Captain agreed. "Now, here is the plan worked out by the Mayor, the Police Chief, and myself. President McKinley will have a private train from Washington by way of Chicago. When his train arrives at Union Station in downtown Omaha, he will be met by a delegation of prominent local citizens. The President and other dignitaries will be delivered to a specially constructed grandstand in front of the Court House, which will be highly illuminated with electric lights, should the event be after dark. There will be a grand parade, which will undoubtedly be attended by thousands of local residents, as well as visitors to the Exposition. He will then be feted with a dinner at the elegant Omaha Club, where a special room will be prepared for his lodging. Next day, he will speak at the Exposition. And on the following day, he will embark for Washington once again on his special train."

"And all we have to do is protect him," I grunted, "on a schedule that would afford would-be assassins a thousand easy opportunities."

"I beg your pardon," Captain Lewellen bristled.

"Dr. Watson is quite right, of course," Sherlock Holmes agreed. I confess that I felt quite proud. "But your plan should be put into effect, and made known to the newspapers."

"But Holmes," I protested. "This is nothing short of handing the President over to his enemies."

"See here," Captain Lewellen replied. "A great deal of planning has gone into this. There will be policemen at every intersection. Mounted police will flank the President's carriage. The Omaha Club will be surrounded by police around the clock to make certain that President McKinley will be as safe as if he were in his own bed."

"And he would be most fortunate to survive the night," I observed.

"The Exposition as well as the City has been a beehive of spy activity," Holmes said. "Teams of agents from both Spain and its Cuban toadies have been rotating in and out of town. And you can be assured that whatever actual attack is planned will be carried out by an entirely new team that specializes in such skullduggery. We will not be able to recognize these experts on sight alone."

"Then what do you propose, Holmes?" I asked.

"For the moment," he said, "to circulate the President's itinerary and the Captain's security plans to the general public just as quickly as possible.

The summer wore on with still no word that assured a visit from President McKinley.

Holmes grew more and more restless with each passing day. The man had an appetite for adventure that had to be constantly fed, or his very being began to deteriorate. He often played his violin well into the night. Most disturbing of all to me, however, was his sudden lack of interest in the widow's most excellent cooking. I felt quite certain that he was beginning to treat his lethargy with that accursed cocaine.

"Did you hear Mr. Holmes serenading me again last night?" the widow Thoms asked me, as I sat at the breakfast table one morning in mid-July. "My first husband, God rest his soul, just was not a romantic like my Sherlock."

"I assure you, dear madam, no one is a romantic like Sherlock Holmes," I muttered.

"Playing love songs on his violin to his be-trothed," the widow beamed, clasping her hands to her most ample bosoms and rolling her eyes back-ward, "is the most tender expression of love that I could possibly imagine."

"If anything can possibly be imagined, dear lady," I sighed, "you are certainly my personal choice for the task."

"And did you notice how his appetite has slack-ened, Dr. Watson?"

"I daresay, I have," I replied. "But what could that possibly have to do with his violin renditions?"

"You know what they say?" she tittered. "Young people in love are never hungry."

"Since I am neither young nor in love," I said with scarcely disguised irritation, "I should apprec-iate it if you would prepare my usual ration of bacon and eggs. For I assure you that I am quite hungry."

"How inconsiderate of me," the widow said,

rushing to prepare my food. "It's just that I am so excited. I just can't wait for September. Can you?"

"I most assuredly can," I replied. But nothing could calm the ardor of the widow Thoms.

The war continued to go well for America, with the Spanish surrender of Cuba in mid-July. Porto Rico was promptly invaded, and by late July, Spain officially sued for peace. Heavy fighting continued in the Philippines, however, where tropic diseases were taking heavier American casualties than the enemy. When Manila finally surrendered on August 16th, Mayor Moores decided that it was time to send a delegation to Washington to pressure President McKinley to name a date for his visit. An oil painting of the Exposition Grand Court by the grandson of Francis Scott Key was presented to McKinley as an inducement. On August 21st, the word finally came through. President McKinley would visit Omaha and the Trans-Mississippi Exposition some time in October. He could not come sooner, because the peace talks in Paris would not begin until October 1st.

A renewed flurry of activity began in both Omaha and at the Exposition. Construction began immediately on a large viewing stand in front of the Court House downtown. A few blocks away, a crew of workmen busily remodeled a main floor room of the elegant Omaha Club which would serve as a bedroom for the President. The main floor party room was bedecked in red, white and blue, as well as the green, yellow and red flags of the Knights of Aksarben. This most exclusive club of Omaha's finest literally operated the City, behind their clever name which was concocted by spelling "Nebraska" backwards.

Exposition leaders decided to bill the President's visit as a celebration of "Peace Jubilee", even though the war was not officially over, and in fact skirmishes were still being fought in the Philippines. The Exposition grounds and buildings were festooned with banners and flags. New gardens were planted by the Exposition's ever busy nurserymen, who arranged the flower beds as replicas of the American flag as well as patriotic slogans. "Cuba libra" and "Remember the Maine" were most prominent.

The last day of August was particularly memorable for both Holmes and myself. It was designated "Old Timer's Day", and the guest of honor was none other than Buffalo Bill Cody. The regularly featured "Wild West Show" on the Midway was dedicated to him. And nothing could have been deemed more appropriate. For as Mr. Cody himself explained, he had personally held the world's first "Wild West Show" some fifteen years earlier on the very bluff tract now occupied by the Midway. I have rarely seen Sherlock Holmes as impressed as when he shook the hand of Buffalo Bill.

As September was being born, the President still had not announced an exact date for his visit. However, the exact date of the Thoms-Holmes nuptials was virtually upon us. Try as I might, I could not convince Holmes of the widow's intentions. Nor could the widow's elan be curbed by insinuations that Sherlock Holmes was not marriageable.

With the wedding one short week away, and with my nerves fairly in shreds, I resolved to lose it all in the morning paper over my favorite breakfast. The intrigues of Madam Dreyfus in Paris were indeed a diversion, especially since the great Emile

Zola had risen to her defense. Then there were reports of continued scattered fighting in the Philippines. However, it was when I leafed over to page four of "The Morning Bee" that I discovered the greatest news to me personally.

"Eureka," I shouted, with no less enthusiasm than the Greek scientist.

"What is it?" Mrs. Thoms asked, rushing into the kitchen.

"This news item," I shouted. "I shall read it to you. 'It was brought to the attention of your editor that a most untoward incident occurred last night at Grace Episcopal Church.' "

"Why — that's the Church where Mr. Holmes and I are to be married next Saturday,"

"It seems that the Reverend Wickham, rector of the Church, was conducting a Saturday night prayer service for the ladies of the Church, when a huge chandelier broke loose from the ceiling.'"

"Oh dear," Mrs. Thoms said. "I do hope that no one was injured."

"Fortunately," I read on, "the group was in a prayer circle at the time of the incident, and the chandelier crashed in the center of the circle. However, flaming fluid from the many shattered lamps splashed on to several of the most shocked ladies, setting fire to their lacy Sunday bests."

"How horrible," the widow exclaimed.

"However," the article continued, " Father Wickham was both quick of mind and hand. He saved the day by the prompt laying on of hands on the ladies, speedily squelching the fires before they could burn the skin."

"How heroic," Mrs. Thoms rejoiced.

"Some of the ladies so treated," I read on,

"reported that they did not recall their clothes being on fire in the first place, but were grateful for the Reverend's ministering in any event."

At that point, there was a heavy knocking at the front door. Before the widow could answer it, the Reverend Wickham came bursting into our presence. "Mrs. Thoms," he panted, "you will never guess what has happened."

"The Church caught on fire," she replied.

"Why — you are positively psychic," the Priest exclaimed.

"It was in the morning paper," I replied dryly.

"Oh," Father Wickham said somewhat disappointedly. "In any case, widow Thoms, I am afraid that this somewhat throws cold water on your wedding plans."

"Why so?" Mrs. Thoms enquired.

"The sanctuary is badly damaged," the Reverend Wickham said sadly. "According to our contractor, it will be six weeks time before the damage is repaired."

"Six weeks?" I rejoiced.

"Six weeks?" the widow moaned.

"This time it will be equipped with electric lighting," the Reverend said emphatically. "You know, I have been preaching electric lighting to the vestry for months. But no one listens to the rector."

"Around here," I observed, "no one listens to anyone."

"Perhaps you could get married by another clergyman," Father Wickham said somewhat apologetically.

"No, no." I protested. "That would never do. Why, Holmes considers you a giant in the field of religion. In fact, you have become his spiritual leader."

"I had no idea," Father Wickham said in dismay. "I don't recall seeing him in Church."

"He is a master of disguise," I explained.

"That's true," Mrs. Thoms confirmed.

"He has been to your Church every Sunday," I lied, "sometimes disguised as an old man, sometimes as a doctor."

"We don't get too many doctors," the Reverend sighed wistfully.

"Only once as a doctor," I quickly amended. "But most every Sunday evening, Holmes comes to my room, and we discuss every nuance of your sermon, sometimes well into the night."

"How very rewarding," Father Wickham beamed.

"Rewarding indeed," I replied. "For both of us. No, no, Father Wickham. Sherlock Holmes would consent to no one but you performing his marriage ceremony."

"I have it," the widow said with great inspiration. "You are currently holding Sunday services in a neighboring Church building, according to the newspaper article."

"True," the Priest concurred.

"Surely they would agree to loan us the use of their facilities for our wedding as well," she suggested happily.

"Of course," Wickham clapped his hands. "Whyever didn't I think of that?"

"Out of the question," I hastened. "Holmes first became enamored with your edifice because it was virtually a replica of his childhood Church in England," I lied, "where as a lad he served as an altar-boy. No, no — it must be your Church. I assure you that Holmes is adamant on the subject."

"But," Mrs. Thoms said with dismay, "it will take six weeks to repair the Church. Do you think that Mr. Holmes can wait six weeks?"

"He has waited thirty-six years, widow Thoms," I assured her. "Please take my word for it. He can indeed survive another six weeks."

Such blatant prevarication to a man of the cloth smote my conscience, I confess, but only briefly. Holmes was reprieved for another six weeks, which hopefully should prove sufficient. The news of the next few days all but confirmed this.

On September 7th, "The Morning Bee" proclaimed the President's decision. He would arrive in Omaha on October 11th, visit the Exposition on the twelfth, and leave for Washington on the thirteenth.

CHAPTER EIGHTEEN

About ten days later, I came down from my room as usual for breakfast. The widow informed me that Sherlock Holmes left word for me to attend a breakfast meeting with him and Captain Lewellen at the "Bohemian Inn" restaurant on the Midway at the Exposition.

I stepped out on the porch to hail a hack, when I realized what beautiful early fall day it was. So I decided to walk the four blocks to the Exposition grounds. On the way, I purchased a copy of "The Morning Bee" from a newspaper lad. The little scoundrel was so distrustful, that he refused to give me my newspaper until he had my five-cent piece safely in his pocket.

I read the headlines and some of the articles, as I ambled toward the Exposition gates. The whining of the electric streetcars mingled with the clopping of horses hooves on the brick pavement and the train whistles below the bluff, as all three modes of transportation bore loads of the first patrons of the day to the Exposition.

The news of the day indicated that the Trans-Mississippi Exposition was now totally out of debt. There was news that many of President McKinley's cabinet members would visit the Exposition with him, as well as a number of heroes from the on-going war. Peace talks between Spain and America would begin October 1st in Paris. And young Teddy Roosevelt, the reckless hero of San Juan Hill, was nominated for Governor of the State of New York.

"Unbelievable," I muttered. "If he had led the 'Charge of the Light Brigade', Americans would probably have crowned him king for such foolhardy behavior."

The newspaper also contained details of the President's schedule upon his arrival in Omaha, as well as a complete description of the security measures that would supposedly protect him. These, I might add, were equally unbelievable.

Sherlock Holmes and Captain Lewellen were already eating breakfast when I arrived at the "Bohemian Inn". I am happy to report that Holmes' appetite, although not voracious, was indeed becoming healthy once again.

"My dear Watson," Holmes greeted me amiably. "Do join us." He beckoned to the waitress, who promptly brought me a most handsome portion of my favorite morning food. "I took the liberty of ordering for you. I do hope that you don't object."

"Most certainly not," I exclaimed. "I couldn't be more delighted."

"Very well," Holmes said. "Now, down to business. The article in the morning papers was outstanding, Captain Lewellen. So far, you have done your part in this matter very well indeed."

"Thank you," the Captain replied with pride.

"Well indeed?" I said credulously, nearly choking on a rasher of bacon. "Holmes, you know very well that this plan is setting the President up for murder."

"Exactly," Holmes replied. "Now the Spanish and Cuban agents can begin working in earnest on how best to plan their attack."

"Aren't we playing into their hands?" I asked.

"Not really," Holmes explained. "Actually, they will be playing into ours. You see, President McKinley will never be in downtown Omaha."

"Holmes," I said impatiently, "I don't believe that you have read the article in this morning's newspaper."

"I didn't have to," Holmes replied. "I wrote it. And Captain Lewellen was clever enough to let it fall into the hands of our local newpaper editors."

"You see, Dr. Watson," Captain Lewellen explained, "although a large reviewing stand is being built in front of the Court House, President McKinley will never sit in it."

"And," Sherlock Holmes went on, "although the elegant Omaha Club has been elaborately decorated, the President will not be feted there."

"Nor," Captain Lewellen said, "will he sleep in the room that has been totally refurbished in his honor."

"Then where in the name of Queen Victoria will the President be?" I asked in dismay.

"Here at the Exposition," the Captain beamed.

"But — how?" I asked, totally ignoring my breakfast, which by now was beginning to get cold.

"When the President's train leaves Chicago," Sherlock Holmes began, "there will be a military train preceding his train, and another following it. I personally don't believe that an attempt will be made on his life while crossing the Great Plains, but considering the state of the world, we cannot take chances."

"When the trains arrive in Omaha," Captain Lewellen continued, the President's car will be switched to the track leading to the Exposition grounds."

"Once there," Holmes said, "the President will be housed in a most elegant train car loaned to us by a railroad executive, which is located on the railroad siding by the Exposition's private dignitary entrance. We will have this relatively confined area well-staffed with both the military and Captain Lewellen's Exposition police. He shall be quite safe."

"But," I stammered, "won't the people of Omaha be quite angry when the President fails to appear at the parade?"

"One of the Captain's trusted Lieutenants will make the announcement at the reviewing stand by the Court House, and will personally lead the parade and the people on a march to the gates of the Exposition grounds, where the same festivities will be carried out. I am certain that the good people of Omaha will be willing to walk four miles in order save their President's life."

"So you see, Dr. Watson," the Captain fairly bubbled, "the Spanish and Cuban agents can feel free to position all the assassins they choose, because the President will not be traveling the route they suspect."

"I must confess that I am somewhat relieved," I replied, once again attacking my breakfast with great enthusiasm.

The month of October began with the news that announced the opening of peace negotiations in Paris on the one hand, and renewed raging war in Porto Rico on the other. This caused further worry for those of us pledged to guarantee the safety of President McKinley.

To make tensions even worse, on October 6th, it was reported that a force of eighty soldiers led by General Bacon had been massacred by Indians near Leech Lake in Minnesota. People traveling in trains reported seeing two hundred and fifty armed warriors in full headdress riding towards Bear Island, where the battle was reported to have been fought. Considering the number of Indians performing at the Exposition, including the Great Chief Geronimo, who recently arrived with fifty of his braves, the strain on our Exposition police force was beginning to show. It was not until the day before the President's arrival that news came through that the events in Minnesota were not another Custer-type massacre, although it had the potential for it. Six soldiers, including two officers, had been killed. But the main force had escaped to Bear Island. A military rescue had been made, and the Indians had left the scene, many of them returning to their reservations. As to the resident Indians at the Exposition, if they were aware of the events in Minnesota, they showed no outward signs of it.

CHAPTER NINETEEN

With the President's arrival only one day away, an incident occurred in downtown Omaha that threatened the peace of all North America. Considering the fact that the problems with Spain in the Caribbean Sea were still not totally settled, this event could not have been more untimely.

Tensions between the United States and Mexico regarding the war fought fifty years previously were finally easing. A Mexican businessman, one Juan Lopez, had in fact been sent as a special envoy to the Trans-Mississippi Exposition. Special efforts had been made by Exposition officials not only to make him feel welcome, but also to make him feel very important. A deluxe suite of rooms was provided for him in one of Omaha's finest hotels, courtesy of the Exposition directors. It was hoped that favorable reports would be funneled back to Mexico, further strengthening the new ties of friendship which President McKinley was trying to establish with America's neighbor to its south. Exposition officials were delighted when they learned that five more members had joined Senor Lopez at his hotel, and were particularly happy that they had provided more than enough hotel space to accommodate them all.

When the leader of the delegation, Senor Lopez, was found on the morning of October 10th, murdered in his bed, the other members of his delegation were understandably distressed. This distress turned to outrage when the coroner removed the body, and a message in English under the corpse said, "Remember the Alamo! Death to Mexico!", and was signed with the symbol of the American eagle.

The good relations with the Mexican delegation instantly turned ugly, and the Mexicans lodged a protest with Washington. Police Chief Smith immediately sent apologies to the remaining five delegation members, and the City of Omaha offered to pay funeral expenses.

The body was removed to a local mortuary. Mayor Moores ordered that it be laid-in-state in the most expensive casket available, and personally led a delegation of city officials to pay his respects. From his train, President McKinley wired his sympathies to the delegation, promising to pay his respects personally on October 12th, the day after he would arrive. The Mexican delegation wired back a message of appreciation, but stated that they would be returning the body to Mexico very early on the morning of October 12th, and hence a Presidential visit to the mortuary would be impossible. However,

McKinley's most kind offer seemed to greatly assuage the Mexican delegation.

Much to my surprise, Sherlock Holmes displayed a rare bit of emotionalism, by insisting that he, myself and Captain Lewellen present our own condolences to the deceased and his compatriots at the mortuary. The fact that it was the eve of the arrival of the President made it seem even more incongruous. However, not being one to discourage even a spark of kindness in a fellow human being, I readily acquiesced. I was somewhat amazed when Holmes rather emotionally bowed his head over the corpus in what appeared to be solemn prayer, then shook the hand of each of the deceased's comrades, while offering his most sincere sympathy. Captain Lewellen and I, of course, did the same.

"What was that all about?" I asked, with obvious suspicion.

"My dear Watson," Holmes replied, "even I feel a responsibility to do my bit toward preserving international tranquility. In fact, as a part of my concern, I intend to send a wire to Albany, New York, tonight."

Tuesday, October 11th, finally dawned. "The Morning Bee" promised that the Presidential train would be departing Chicago late that afternoon, and arrive at Union Station in Omaha a little after nine o'clock in the evening. In fact, I learned later, it had already left about mid-morning. Through some military mix-up, Sherlock Holmes' instructions had been totally ignored. Instead of being flanked by trainloads of military men, the President's train was totally unguarded from the front. And contrary to Holmes' instructions for a rapid trip, President McKinley ordered his train stopped at every hamlet, where he proceeded to deliver speeches from the rear of his car. That the man was not assassinated a hundred times over, could only be attributed to the fact that no enemy agent contemplated such stupidity on the part of his protectors. The Presidential train arrived in Omaha a few minutes earlier than scheduled at about 9:30 that evening.

Captain Lewellen and Lieutenant Holmes had busied themselves throughout the day with security matters at the Exposition grounds. Trackage was cleared so that the Presidential train could be pulled to within a few feet of the luxury train car that would provide McKinley with a home for the next two days. The car itself was inspected several times, both inside and out, to make certain that no explosive devices had somehow been smuggled in.

Holmes had even insisted that a spare locomotive with full crew be stationed on the siding, so that the Presidential train car could be returned safely to Union Station on the morning that McKinley was to depart for Washington.

Several soldiers patrolled a wide area around the Exposition grounds, questioning and searching everyone they encountered. All one hundred Exposition policemen were pressed into service. After the Exposition was closed early in anticipation of the President's supposed arrival downtown, Captain Lewellen's men fairly scoured the grounds to make certain that no potential miscreant had somehow managed to linger. Sherlock Holmes' plan for total security for the President was in place. All we had to do was wait for the arrival of President McKinley's train.

The vigil proved to be longer than we anticipated. As 9:30 approached, Holmes became increasingly agitated.

"Blast it, Watson," he exclaimed. "That train should have been here fifteen minutes ago. I fear that something has gone awry."

"Perhaps the Presidential train was delayed," I ventured feebly. "Such things do happen."

"The last communication we had indicated that it was on time," Holmes said. "No, gentlemen. Someone has veered from our plan."

"What shall we do?" Captain Lewellen asked. "Should I send a contingent of men downtown to survey the situation?"

"I don't think that will be necessary," Holmes replied. "Unless my eyes and intuition fail me, that lone rider galloping up the street towards us is the man who was supposed to lead the parade to the Exposition grounds."

As usual, Holmes proved to be correct. Both the young man and his horse were fairly wind-broken by the time he dismounted and saluted the Captain and Sherlock Holmes.

"I'm sorry, Sirs," he panted, "to report — that the President — insisted — on following — the plan as outlined in this morning's — newspapers."

"What?" Captain Lewellen shouted.

"That is suicide," I exclaimed.

"What caused him to change our plan?" Holmes demanded.

"It seems that President McKinley loves crowds," the young man said. "He had been stop-ping his train at every small town from here to Chicago, they say."

"Why didn't you report sooner?" Captain Lewellen said tersely.

"I've been riding against surging crowds for the past half-hour," the man reported. "There must be two hundred thousand people in the streets of downtown. My horse tripped over people and fell down three times."

"Where is President McKinley now?" Holmes asked.

"The last I saw, the parade had ended, and he was being driven to the Omaha Club," the lad replied.

"Quick, Captain," Holmes instructed. "Summon your carriage. Perhaps with a great deal of luck, we can still manage to transport the President safely back to the Exposition grounds."

Moments later, our carriage was hurtling down Twentieth Street at juggernaut speed, toward downtown Omaha. On two occasions, our carriage wheels wedged into the streetcar tracks, and nearly overturned us. The milling crowds forced us to abandon our carriage about two blocks from the Omaha Club. Holmes was positively magnificent as he battered a path for us through the sea of humanity. All that was required of Captain Lewellen and myself was to stay close behind him. Still and all, it took a full fifteen minutes for us to burrow our way to the front door of that posh establishment, where a policeman promptly stopped us.

"Sorry, gents," he said with a wave of his club. "Nobody gets in without an invitation."

"Is Police Chief Smith on the premises?" Holmes inquired.

"Indeed he is," the officer replied. "But he's much too busy to be bothered at the moment."

"I'm sure he is," Holmes said. "Nevertheless, I feel certain that he will want to know that Lieutenant Holmes of the Exposition Police is here."

"Lieutenant Holmes!" the officer exclaimed. "I'm sorry. I didn't recognize you. And of course, Dr. Watson, as well. You fellows did a splendid job for us on the monastery caper."

"How nice of you to remember," I replied. "Now if you will be kind enough to step aside."

"I'm sorry, Dr. Watson," the policeman said. "Considering the circumstances, I will have to clear your entry with Police Chief Smith." So saying, he disappeared into the building.

"Whatever circumstances could he be alluding to?" I queried. As if in answer to my questions, Police Chief Smith appeared at the door.

"Holmes," he said with patient agitation. "Thank God you're here. Come in quickly — all three of you." Once inside, the Chief wiped his brow with a handkerchief. "You will never guess what has happened." But before we could guess, he provided the answer to his own question. "President McKinley has been assassinated."

"Good heavens," I exclaimed. Even though our greatest fears had been confirmed, I nevertheless was astonished. The murder of a President is an overwhelming event.

"How did it occur?" Sherlock Holmes asked.

"A small party was held for the President," Chief Smith replied. "He ate a small dinner, then complained of being tired. So I escorted him to his room."

"Did the food disagree with him?" I asked.

"If it did," Chief Smith replied, "he didn't complain about it."

"Do go on," Holmes prodded him.

"I personally searched the room that was specially provided for the President," Chief Smith said. "Two of my men assisted me, and they will vouch that the room was secure. About twenty minutes after we left the President to retire, a shot rang out from his bedroom. We rushed back in, and President McKinley was lying on his back next to his bed, his chest and stomach a river of blood, his eyes wide with sudden death."

"Have you removed the body?" Holmes asked.

"We haven't touched a thing," Chief Smith replied. "We are trying to keep this from the press as long as possible."

"Excellent idea," Holmes agreed. "Have you searched the premises?"

"Every room," the Chief said, "the instant the shot was fired. There was no one in the building who was not authorized and above suspicion. The only untoward event was a slightly inebriated member of the catering crew. But his fellow workers quickly tended to him, and got him out of sight."

"Did you search the basement as well?" Holmes asked.

"Absolutely," Chief Smith replied. "We have also searched the roof. The only other action I have taken was to dispatch a man to the Exposition grounds to summon you and Dr. Watson."

"Very good," Holmes nodded. "Now, if you will kindly lead us to the murder scene."

As we followed the Chief, he remarked, "My theory is that someone managed to install a secret panel in the ceiling of the President's bedroom. Then, when President McKinley laid down to rest, the assassin shot the President from the room above, replaced the secret panel, and jumped from the second story window, and made good his escape.

Of course, he would have had to be extremely fortunate not have been seen by my guards outside."

"Did you find such a secret panel?" Captain Lewellen asked.

"No," the Chief admitted. "But I have a team of detectives inspecting the ceiling, and another looking at the floor of the room above. This is the President's room here." Two uniformed policemen who were guarding the door stepped aside, and we entered the room.

No expense had been spared in preparing the Presidential quarters. Queen Victoria herself would have been pleased to celebrate her recent seventy-fifth birthday in such elegance. Luxuriant draperies covered almost every wall. The rich carpeting underfoot seemed to be several inches thick. The huge round bed that graced the center of the room was obviously custom-made for the President. The large splash of blood on the expensive quilt that covered it was a grizzly contrast, as was the body that lay next to it, staring glassy-eyed at the detectives who stood on ladders, inspecting the ceiling with magnifying glasses. Sounds of flooring being torn up echoed from the room above.

Sherlock Holmes immediately stopped over the purple-robed figure on the floor, leaned over the head, and announced, "President McKinley is not dead!"

"What?" Chief Smith said in amazement.

"See here, Holmes," I admonished him. "Being a man of medicine, I can assure you even from this distance that the President is most decidedly quite dead."

"You are quite correct on one point, my dear Watson," Holmes replied. "This man is indeed quite dead. But I doubt seriously if he was ever President of anything, let alone the United States. From the smell of his mouth, my guess is that he is a local drunkard, whose pay for this evening's activities was a bottle of whiskey."

"But," Chief Smith shook his head in disbelief, "I escorted President McKinley to his room personally."

"Indeed you did," Holmes agreed. "And although there is a decided resemblance, this is not the man you left in this room."

"Then where is President McKinley?" I asked.

"My guess is that he has been kidnapped," Holmes replied.

"Then how — and for that matter, why — would anyone switch this man for the President, and then kill him?" I queried.

"That is a mystery we shall soon hope to solve," Holmes answered. He then turned his attention to the fatal wound. "Hello, what's this? Chief Smith, does my memory serve me correctly, or did you say earlier that you heard a single shot coming from this room?"

"That's correct," Chief Smith said. The other detectives in the room verified this information. "Why do you ask?"

"Because there are two wounds," Holmes replied, "one in the chest and the other in the abdomen." I looked, and indeed Holmes was correct.

"Someone really wanted this fellow dead," I observed. "Either wound would have been quite sufficient."

"I doubt," Holmes said, "that anyone wanted this person dead."

"Then there were two assassins," Captain Lewellen suggested, "who fired the shots simultaneously."

"Or a two-gunned assassin," I offered. "There are certainly a number of such experts performing daily at the Exposition's 'Wild West Show'."

"Both are interesting theories," Holmes replied. "Unfortunately, neither is correct." Then he said to the two detectives on the ladders, "You gentlemen can stop examining the ceiling now, since there is nothing up there to discover. Chief Smith, can you get me the names of the contractors who remodelled this room? And the plans that they worked from as well, if possible, although I seriously doubt that either will prove helpful."

"The Omaha Club President is in the building at present," the Chief replied. "One of you men please summon him directly."

"And the other please tell the detectives upstairs to stop removing the floor boards," Holmes added. "They have already caused quite enough damage to these elegant premises."

"If Dr. Watson's and my theories are wrong," Captain Lewellen asked, "then how do you explain the disappearance of President McKinley and the murder of this man?"

"Yes," I concurred. "What group would want to perpetrate such a strange series of events?"

"Not 'group', Watson," Holmes explained. "It would be more accurate to say 'groups'."

"I don't understand," Captain Lewellen admitted.

"My guess is that the President of the Omaha Club will confirm that one contractor provided the construction alterations for this room as well as the adjoining kitchen, and that a second contractor supplied the furnishings. I would also wager that both contractors submitted bids that were ridiculously low, in order to be assured of getting the jobs."

"Absolutely correct on both counts," a voice said from behind me. "Hello. I'm Ashley Schafer, President of the Omaha Club."

"Charmed," I acknowledged.

"And I presume that each claimed the low bid would provide excellent future advertising, since they could then associate themselves with President McKinley," Holmes went on.

"Right once again," Mr. Schafer nodded.

"I would wager also," Holmes continued, "that the remodelling contractors catered the Presidential Party tonight, or at the very least, arranged to have it catered, also at a very reasonable price."

"That is correct," Mr. Schafer replied. "But I can assure you that the food was of excellent quality, and was even sampled before it was served to make certain that the President's health was never in danger."

"And I can assure you," Police Chief Smith added, "that no weapons of any kind were smuggled into the building, since my men and myself searched every container and cart that was brought in."

"Nevertheless," Holmes said, "these people were your kidnappers."

"In that case," Chief Smith snapped, "give me their names, and I will have them investigated immediately."

"The names are fictitious," Holmes replied. "Thank you for your trouble, Mr. Schafer."

"If I can be of further help, please ask."

With the departure of Mr. Schafer, Holmes began reconstructing the crime. "There is some clandestine entrance to this room, on the west wall about here," he announced. "Note how the extra thick carpet is well-matted down, which is hardly to be expected against a wall, even when you have as many bunglers destroying evidence as we have had in this room tonight."

"But — where is the entrance?" Captain Smith asked.

"That we shall soon discover," Holmes replied. " In any case, our kidnappers have such a lead on us now, that thoroughness is more of the essence than time. Now, Chief Smith, let us presume that you and your men have just searched this room. Finding it secure, you bid President McKinley a good night, and leave the room, shutting that door. Our kidnappers emerge instantly from their clandestine hiding place behind this wall. They chloroform the President, remove him through the same secret door, and replace him with this thoroughly soused substitute, clothing him in the President's night robe."

"But — why?" I asked.

"To gain time," Holmes replied. "Had this fellow not been shot, no one would have been the wiser. Even had Chief Smith felt it necessary to check on the President from time to time during the night, this chap's numbed carcass lying on the bed in the President's robe would have convinced him that the President, who had already complained of being tired, was merely sleeping."

"It was my intent to look in on him several times," Chief Smith nodded. "And I most certainly would have been fooled."

"By the time this poor fellow sobered up," Holmes said, "our kidnappers would have had President McKinley well on his way to some yet to be determined destination."

"Cuba, perhaps?" I ventured.

"Perhaps," Holmes replied. "Spain has so thoroughly lost the war with America, that it stands to lose everything at the peace talks currently being held in Paris. But the so-called 'Dons' — the resident large landowners of Cuba, who have prospered so well under their Spanish occupiers — are a different story. By holding President McKinley for ransom, they might well hold a much better bargaining position at the peace talks, and be able to retain much of their present wealth and power."

"Then," I asked, "why was this poor devil murdered in cold blood?"

"As I just said," Holmes explained. "Spain in any event stands to lose everything at the peace talks in Paris. So what does that leave them? Revenge. The Spaniards wanted President McKinley dead."

"But — how did they get in?" I asked.

"Or out, for that matter?" Chief Smith queried. "I can assure you, this building has been guarded to the extreme."

"They were 'in' when this room was refurbished," Holmes said. "You will note extensive powder burns around the wounds of our victim. This indicates that the shots were fired at extremely close range."

"But how?" I asked.

"From two revolvers implanted in the mattress of that custom-made bed," Holmes announced. So saying, he pulled back the blood-soaked bedspread to reveal two holes the mattress. "When you dissect this mattress, Chief Smith, you will find two revolvers pointing upward, rigged to fire when a weight of one hundred and fifty pounds or more is placed on it. Some sort of timing device will be attached that would prevent such a thing from happening before this evening. Two revolvers were required because of the huge size of the bed, so that one or the other would be sure to kill the President. This chap was unfortunate enough to get both of them."

"Marvelous," I said.

"Elementary, actually," Holmes shrugged. "Now, continuing on with the reconstruction of the crime. Our kidnappers have removed the drugged President from this room to a secret room behind the wall, which I daresay also abuts the kitchen. There he was placed in one of the now empty food carts used to cater the Presidential party, and wheeled out past your guards without anyone suspecting a thing. You see, Chief Smith, your presumption was that something might be smuggled into the building. So everything that came in was carefully searched. In reality, our enemy guessed correctly that no one would search something that appeared to be legitimately removed from the building."

"A clever lot indeed," I observed.

"And it may well have worked," Sherlock Holmes said. "My guess is that our victim, after he had been wrapped in the President's night robe and left alone, probably combed the room in search of more alcoholic spirits. After twenty minutes or so of fruitless seeking, he undoubtedly felt the need of sleep. He stumbled over to the bed, and threw himself face down on it. Both revolvers fired simultaneously, sounding as the single shot you heard, into his chest and abdomen. The force of the shots blew his body off of the bed, landing him on his back next to the bed, already quite dead. Come, let us go inspect the kitchen." Holmes immediately led us through the Club as if he had been there a hundred times before. His path took us in a basic circle into the area where food was prepared. He quickly located a secret door which opened into a cubicle that would hold three or four people. A simple latch opened a wall panel, which placed us once again back into the Presidential bedroom. "Well, Watson," Holmes observed with what could be considered inappropriate enthusiasm, "we now know how they did it and why they did it. Now all we have to do is deduce who they are, where they have taken him, and then rescue him — and all before his scheduled appearance at the Exposition tomorrow."

"I'm glad that you are so confident," Captain Lewellen grunted.

"Chief Smith," Holmes instructed, "it is of the utmost importance that no word be circulated about the events of this evening. The Spaniard assassins have probably long since departed the area. But in the event they have not, they may attempt to return to learn why no news was forthcoming on the President's assassination. Also, we want the kidnappers to believe that no one as yet even suspects that President McKinley has been abducted."

"Consider it done," Chief Smith replied. "I shall quarantine the Omaha Club indefinitely. With the exception of police personnel, which of course includes you and Dr. Watson, no one shall be permitted to enter or leave the building."

CHAPTER TWENTY

At Sherlock Holmes' request, Captain Lewellen drove us back to the Exposition grounds, where we went promptly to the telegraph room at the Fire and Police building.

"I am expecting a wire from New York," Holmes said to the clerk behind the counter.

"It arrived a few minutes ago, Lieutenant Holmes," the man replied. Holmes took the wire, and retired to a chair across the room, where he began to read it. "By the way, Captain Lewellen. I'm afraid that we have yet another international incident on our hands. One of our Exposition guards found what appears to be the body of yet another Mexican national. We have brought it up to the Exposition hospital."

"Great heavens, no," Lewellen exclaimed. "We are going to be at war with Mexico as well as Spain in no time at all."

"Where was the body found?" I asked.

"Why don't you ask Private Kirk about the details," the clerk suggested. "He's the man who found the body, and he is right over there by Lieutenant Holmes." Captain Lewellen and I immediately went over to Private Kirk.

"We need the details of this latest murder of a Mexican, Private," Captain Lewellen said. "Where did you find the body?"

"I pulled it from the river below the bluff," the private replied. "Naked as a newborn baby. We have no idea who he is."

"Has the Mayor been informed?" Lewellen asked.

"We have sent word to him," Private Kirk replied, "and to Police Chief Smith as well." Throughout all of this exchange, Sherlock Holmes merely sat and read his wire.

"For heavens sake, Holmes," I said somewhat irritably. "Aren't you the least bit concerned about this latest dastardly development?"

"What's that?" he asked somewhat distractedly. "Oh, yes, Watson. Of course, I am. By the way, Private, did the body by any chance have its hands folded on its chest?"

"As a matter of fact, it did," Private Kirk said with amazement. "How did you know?"

"When did you find the body?" Holmes asked.

"About an hour ago," the Private replied.

"When you pulled the body from the water, did you by any chance note any boating activity on the river at the time?" Holmes asked.

"Only an old steamboat," Private Kirk answered. "It was like one of those boats that used to bring all the supplies up the Missouri, before the trains put most of them out of business."

"Do steamboats normally travel the river at night?" Holmes queried.

"Now that you mention it, it is pretty unusual," the Private said. "I hear tell that a lot of steamboats ran aground and sank in this part of the river back in the '80s."

"But there is a new moon out," Captain Lewellen ventured. "So navigation should not be too difficult."

"What in the name of Queen Victoria has this to do with our mysterious murders?" I exploded. "Great heavens, Holmes, we have more important things to discuss than moonlight on the river."

"I'm afraid that you are quite wrong, my dear Watson," Holmes smiled. "Captain Lewellen, do you have a map of this general area?"

"There's one on the wall of the conference room," the Captain said. We followed the Captain to the map, which Holmes studied briefly.

"Would it be possible," Holmes asked, "to switch a train onto this C.B. & Q. Railroad line at the yards downtown?"

"Of course," Captain Lewellen said. "But why would we want to do that?"

"To rescue the President, of course," Holmes said calmly. "This village of Bellevue, several miles to the south — does it have a railroad siding of some sort?"

"I'm sure it does," the Captain said with obvious bewilderment. "All of these small towns have at least one."

"Very well," Holmes said. "Send a courier to alert our locomotive crew at the Exposition railroad siding. Have them hook up to the President's car and be prepared to leave immediately. Have one of your best riders mount your fastest horse and ride to Union Station. He is to instruct the stationmaster to have a direct route switched through so that we can proceed without delay to the Bellevue Station."

"Aren't you going to inspect the body of our latest victim first?" I queried.

"I already have inspected it," Holmes answered. "Come, Watson. And you, too, Captain. We have a train to catch." Holmes paused only long enough to send a wire to the Bellevue Station.

The three of us left in Captain Lewellen's carriage from the Fire and Police building on the main court. The bright light of the new moon illuminated the ornate facades of the many buildings with an eerie beauty that surpassed the electric lights that so impressed most evening visitors to the Exposition. The horses crossed the viaduct, then clattered up the brick road toward the bluff tract. At Holmes' direction, we made one small side-trip to "The Big Rock" attraction on the Midway. While Holmes visited with the gypsy dancer who had created the "Devil's Dance", my mind wandered back to that day when we captured Colonel Huston, alias the "Chameleon". I recalled being so enthralled with the dance production, with its torrential rains and walls of fire, that I had briefly forgotten about the chase.

I was shaken from my reverie, when Holmes returned to the carriage with the gypsy. Both were heavily laden with boxes, which they loaded on to the rear of the carriage. They climbed aboard, and Captain Lewellen once again urged the horses forward.

By the time that Captain Lewellen's carriage

pulled up at the siding, the train crew was already coupling the President's special car behind the engine and fuel car. Our gypsy companion loaded his paraphernalia on board, and moments later we were gliding down the bluff to the river bank below. As we weaved our way through the maze of tracks that abutted the Missouri River, Holmes read his telegram to us.

"To the Honorable Sherlock Holmes: My fondest regards. The insignia you described in your telegram is well-known to me. It is indelibly stamped on the wrists of members of a radical group of Cuban aristrocrats who are determined that Cuba will not be liberated by the United States. They will stop at nothing to achieve their goal. If you encounter any of this group, be especially careful. I hope this information is of some help to you. Please visit me in New York, if you can, on your way back to England. If you arrive after Election Day, you will find me in the Governor's Mansion. Best regards. Signed, Theodore Roosevelt."

By now, our train had reached the labyrinth that comprised the Union Station yard. Switchmen were stationed out in front of us making the necessary track changes that would lead us to the C.B. & Q. Railroad, and ultimately to the village of Bellevue.

"What has that tatoo to do with our victim?" Captain Lewellen asked. "He didn't have any insignia on his wrist."

"But all of his comrades do indeed have it," Holmes said. "I checked each of their wrists while giving my condolences at the mortuary."

"I should have guessed that you weren't suffering a burst of sentimentality," I grunted. "But what has all of this to do with our latest murder victim?"

"Our latest murder victim is one and the same as our first victim?" Holmes stated.

"How do you know?" Captain Lewellen demanded to know. "You didn't even bother to examine the second body."

"You will recall that the private who found the body reported that it was nude, and that its hands were crossed over its chest. It is common knowledge that morticians do not dress a corpse as such, but rather slit their clothing up the back, and then merely tuck it under the body. To leave a body so clothed would alert anyone to its identity. So it was logical to leave it nude. As to the hands being folded on the chest, this is how the mortician arranged the body for viewing. Rigor mortis being what it is, it would be all but impossible to realign the posture of a corpse after such a long time, and even more impossible to dress it in a normal manner."

"But why would anyone want to dispose of this poor fellow's body in such a way?" I asked.

"Why, indeed," Holmes replied. "I see that our train has finally cleared the railroad yards. We should be picking up speed very soon now." In response to Holmes' words, the train suddenly leaped forward into the moonlit night.

"I have yet to understand why we are racing in a train south from Omaha," Captain Lewellen said, "when we should be trying to locate President McKinley."

"Actually," Holmes replied, "we are racing a steamboat."

"You mean," I asked with disbelief, "the one that Private Kirk sighted below the bluff well over two hours ago?"

"The very one," Holmes nodded.

"Great heavens, Holmes," I shook my head. "It has much too great of a lead on us. I know that steamboats don't travel with much speed, but then neither have we. And the boat is going downstream in any event, which increases its speed all the more."

"If you recall the map on Captain Lewellen's wall," Holmes explained, "the Missouri River travels basically due south until it comes to the town of South Omaha. The steamboat is undoubtedly well past that point by now."

"Then however will we catch it?" I asked.

"And for that matter, why?" the Captain added.

"At South Omaha," Holmes continued patiently, "the river makes an almost right-angle turn, and heads straight east for perhaps five miles. It then takes a short loop, and heads back due west for another five miles to the village of Bellevue. This is a treacherous stretch of river I am told, and a slow one to navigate, even by daylight."

"And why is that significant?" I asked.

"Because our train will be traveling at a high rate of speed across the peninsula created by the long loop in the river. Our train will have to travel only about five miles, while the steamboat is travelling twelve miles. Have no fear, my dear Watson. We will win the race."

Presently we were hurtling through a thick forest, the likes of which I thought could not possibly exist on the Great Plains of the United States. A few minutes later, our train slowed perceptibly, and then inched its way on to a siding next to a desolate little station labelled "Bellevue, Nebraska", where the wheels noisily ground to a halt.

We quickly alit, and were greeted by a hack that

Holmes had wired the stationmaster to have ready. We transferred the gypsy's boxes to it, climbed aboard, and headed due east at a gallop. Before long, we arrived at the edge of the Missouri River, where a good-sized boat was waiting for us. Its crew had obviously been hastily summoned from their beds, but thanks to the handsome wages Holmes had promised for their night's work, there was no grumbling among them.

"What in heaven's name are you planning?" I asked Holmes, as the boatmen began stringing fishing nets together, while our gypsy friend unloaded his boxes.

"As Theodore Roosevelt said in his telegram," Holmes replied, "our adversaries are truly desperate men who will stop at nothing. If we attempt to take them by force, they will most assuredly murder President McKinley without an ounce of remorse, just as they murdered the envoy from Mexico when it became expedient."

"But what has a sideshow performer to do with it?" Captain Lewellen asked.

"If we don't dare risk taking them by force," Sherlock Holmes replied, "then we must take them by deceit."

The gypsy was now tying small packages of material into the fishing nets, spacing them at regular intervals. He connected them with some sort of cord or wire. The net was then loaded into the large boat. One end was tied to the pier on which we were standing. As the boat pulled out, and crossed the river, the fishing net tumbled out of the boat. By the time they had stretched the net across the relatively narrow river channel, a steamboat came around the sharp bend slowly wending its way through the extremely sharp curve. When it was about one hundred yards from our net, Sherlock Holmes nodded to the gypsy, who promptly touched something in a box that was hooked to the wire in the fish netting. Suddenly a wall of fire shot across the river channel, exactly like the one I had viewed in the 'Devil's Dance', rising to a height of seventy feet in the air, which brightly illuminated the river and its banks.

The steamboat immediately veered to the right in order to avoid the flames.

"Have your revolvers ready," Holmes instructed us, as the confused and frightened steamboat captain steered his craft up to our pier. The surprise was so complete, that we were able to capture all five of the kidnappers without firing a shot. The boat captain and his crew were totally unaware that any crimes were being committed, and were completely mystified at our actions.

We quickly searched the vessel, and found no trace of President McKinley.

"I feel somehow," Captain Lewellen stated, "that we have made some ghastly mistake."

"There is no mistake," Holmes said flatly. "These are the men who kidnapped President McKinley."

The flames on the river died as quickly as they had exploded, and our hired boat returned to the pier. The fish netting had been totally consumed by the blast of fire.

"Lieutenant Holmes," the gypsy shouted after conferring with the crew. "I don't know if this is important or not, but just as the steamboat veered to avoid the flames, the crewmen said that they heard something splash in the water."

"Of course!" Holmes fairly shouted. "That is it! Gentlemen, we have further use of your boat." Leaving Captain Lewellen and the gypsy in charge of our prisoners, who were by now securely bound, Holmes and I boarded our hired boat, which immediately chugged out into the river and headed downstream. Holmes stood in the bow like a masculine version of a figurehead on an ancient Viking ship, and peered intently into the moonlit waters ahead.

"Just what is it that we are looking for?" I asked somewhat skeptically. I was beginning to believe that he was losing his mind, and that the United States would spend the next decade apologizing for all of the internationl incidents he had created in one short night.

"Quiet, Watson," he said. "I shall explain everything shortly."

By now, the sky in the east was beginning to grow lighter. The bright moonlight was gradually washed away with the dawn. The light of the new day revealed rich farmland on either bank, some of which was in the process of the fall harvest. I was reflecting on the total inaccuracy of my previous concept of the Great Plains of America, when Holmes jolted my senses to reality by shouting, "There it is!"

"Where is what?" I mumbled, stumbling to my feet.

"There," Holmes pointed, "floating in the water."

I strained my eyes, following the direction that Holmes was indicating. As I realized what I was seeing, my mouth hung open in amazement. I was totally incapable of speech, even as our boat closed in on the object. There, bobbing up and down in the water, steadily working its way downstream, was the elegant casket that we had viewed so recently at the mortuary. Our boat sidled up to it, as Holmes said, "Thank God they drilled air holes in it."

Two of the young crew members grappled it aboard, and Holmes immediately opened it.

"Great heavens," I exclaimed, finally regaining my voice, "It is President McKinley."

"Quite correct," Holmes stated. "And in perfect health, I'll wager."

After a quick examination, I concurred. "Except for the fact that he has been chloroformed, he has not been harmed in any way."

As our crew turned the boat around, and headed back for home port, we removed President McKinley from his ghastly container, and placed him on a cot below. As the boat chugged upstream, we sat by the sleeping President's side, while Sherlock Holmes explained the strange series of events that had led to our present situation.

"The contractor and crew who remodeled the Presidential room at the Omaha Club were agents for the radical Cuban nationals," Holmes explained. "They arranged also to cater the dinner honoring the President, then undoubtedly promptly left town."

"Why so?" I asked.

"So that a new crew of agents, specialists at murder and abduction, could be moved in. They saw an opportunity in the goodwill mission of Senor Lopez from Mexico. They moved in on him at his hotel suite, and convinced everyone that they were part of an extended friendship gesture on the part of the Mexican government."

"And a very convincing job they did," I observed.

"I suspected them of something at the mortu-ary," Holmes went on. "For one thing, they tended to pronounce their 'c' sounds as 'th', which is Casti-lian, whereas your typical Mexican will pronounce them as an 's'. Of course, this is not universal among Mexicans, so it was not conclusive evidence. The symbol tatooed on their wrists intrigued me, and I presumed that Theodore Roosevelt, having recently been deeply involved in the Cuban conflict, could enlighten me on the matter."

"Which indeed he did," I said, "but unfortu-nately not until after President McKinley was kidnapped."

"The Cubans, posing of course as Mexicans, then claimed Senor Lopez' body," Holmes con-tinued, "pretending to be returning it to his home-land. Instead, they dumped it in the river, placed the drugged President in the casket, and proceeded downstream in the steamboat, convinced that no one even suspected that President McKinley was even missing."

"But the murder of the sot who replaced the President was a bit of bad luck for them, I would say," I observed.

"I would have caught on to them in any case," Holmes said. "I had every intention of making cer-tain that the man in the room was indeed the Presi-dent, since I suspected that an abduction had been planned. Ironically, however, it was the abduction that saved President McKinley's life. The revolver traps buried in the mattress by the Spanish agents would most certainly have assassinated him before we ever arrived."

"I can understand the assassination attempt," I said. "Spain will lose an empire because of the war, and might understandably seek revenge. But I fail to comprehend what the Cubans hoped to accomplish with an abduction."

"With Mexico thoroughly angered at the brutal murder of their ambassador of friendship," Holmes explained, "presumably at the hands of the Americans who were unable to forget a war that was fought half a century ago, they hoped to create a new war for the United States."

"I would venture to say that such an event is still a distinct possibility," I observed.

"The capture of our Cuban assassins, along with their speedy trial for the murder of Senor Lopez," Holmes said, "should convince the Mexican government of America's friendship. However, had the Cubans made good their escape, and smuggled President McKinley out of the country in that coffin, the story could have turned out quite differently."

"How so?" I asked.

"With Mexico enraged at the United States," Holmes said, "and the United States without a leader — and, with Cubans physically holding the President as a trump card, the peace negotiators in Paris may well have been forced to recognize the great landholders in Cuba as a legitimate part of a settlement."

"Then they were playing for high stakes indeed," I concluded.

"Indeed they were," Holmes replied. "But fortunately for the world, they lost the game."

President McKinley still had not regained consciousness by the time we arrived back at the pier. The boat crew members carried him to our waiting hack. We shortly joined Captain Lewellen and the gypsy back at the Presidential train. They had already transferred our prisoners to the train, and released the crew of the steamboat after obtaining their promise to testify at the trial. The train crew had during our absence somehow managed to turn the train around. We deposited President McKinley in the bed that, had he chosen to occupy the previous night, would have prevented a great deal of trouble.

As the train rolled north, we once again entered this most amazing forest. Now in full daylight, bathed in the morning sun, I was overwhelmed at the explosion of color around me. Never has the beauty of autumn foliage so impressed me, as the reds and yellows and oranges of the oaks and other trees of this minute but magnificent forest.

We plunged out of this nature wonderland as suddenly as we had entered it, and were once again paralleling the Missouri River. We paused at Union Station only long enough to turn over our five Cuban prisoners to the local police. Chief Smith accepted them, with the remark that we had "fairly overflowed" his local jail with prisoners. It seems that the Spanish assassins, hearing no word of the President being murdered, returned to the Omaha Club to check their trap, and were promptly arrested for the murder of the unfortunate sot.

As the engine was safely depositing our car on the Exposition siding, I was seriously beginning to worry about the President's well-being. He had yet to regain consciousness, which with each passing moment, became a matter of greater concern.

However, as the engine pulled away, and the gypsy departed for his daily performances of the "Devil Dance", the door to the Presidential bedroom opened, and President McKinley stepped out.

"Who — who are you?" he asked in confusion.

"I am Dr. John H. Watson," I replied. "And I would like to introduce you to my colleague, Mr. Sherlock Holmes."

"Of course," President McKinley acknowledged. "I spoke with you on the telephone the opening day of the Exposition. You were brought here to take charge of my security arrangements."

"That is correct, Mr. President," Holmes replied.

"And a first-class job you have done," the President said. "I have never slept so peacefully in my life. Last night I was totally exhausted. In fact, I don't even remember turning in. But now, I feel like a new man."

"Perhaps," I said, "you ought to be made aware of a few details of the night."

But Holmes cut me short, saying, "Why bother President McKinley with such trivial information. However, President McKinley, we have taken the liberty of transferring you to this luxury train car. It is the property of a railroad executive who has loaned it to us for the occasion."

"It's strange," the President said. "I have no recollection of being moved."

"As you observed," Holmes replied, "you were thoroughly exhausted."

"Well," the President said, "I am certainly refreshed now — and exhilarated at the prospect of seeing the Trans-Mississippi Exposition, as well as the thousands of my constituents who will be visiting it. I might add that it is particularly intriguing for me to be so welcomed in the very backyard of my old political adversary, William Jennings Bryan."

"If you are not careful," I warned, "your love of crowds could prove to be your undoing."

When the Exposition gates opened a few hours later, thousands of visitors were already milling behind the turnstyles. All gates were kept busy most of the day. The streetcar company activated all of its electric cars, and still could not meet the demand. By the time a car was within one mile of the Exposition grounds, it was filled to capacity. Those who lived less than a mile away were obliged to walk. I am told that a record crowd of almost one hundred thousand people visited the Exposition that day, and the World's Fair broke the two million visitor mark as well.

The President had lunch at "Caterer Markel's Restaurant", which was located on the viaduct over-looking Sherman Avenue. The weather was marvel-lous, which was well, since the restaurant was open-air, and located high above the mass of humanity that surged below. The President waved happily to the crowd for most of the afternoon, but curbed any urges to make a speech, even though the Congres-sional elections were less than a month away.

The next morning, our engine crew once again hooked up to the President's car, and delivered it to Union Station downtown, where President McKin-ley was transferred to his own train for the trip back to Washington. This time he could no longer contain himself, however, and delivered a speech from the rear of the train. I could only thank the good Lord that all of his enemies were behind bars, because a Presidential assassination would have been an easy matter that morning.

At Holmes' suggestion, those of us who had been privy to the kidnapping of President McKinley agreed to remain silent on the subject. The criminals themselves might do otherwise, but who indeed would believe them? If the world were to know of a Spanish assassination attempt on the President of the United States, the peace talks in Paris might never be settled. Or the people of America might demand an invasion of Spain itself, which almost certainly would ultimately involve all of Europe. Old wounds with Mexico might be re-opened, which could make all of North America into an armed camp or worse for decades to come. The efforts of Colonel Huston to involve the south in yet another disastrous civil war could also upset the further peace of North America.

So you see, now that you have read my journals on this matter, why I felt it so imperative that these memoirs be re-secreted if President McKinley were still in office. That you have read this far proves to me that he is indeed no longer President, and that perhaps sufficient time has elapsed so that revelation of my information would pose no threat to international peace. I can only hope that my suppression of this segment of world history proves to have preserved the tranquility of this planet.

It is now two days after the President's departure to Washington, October 15th, in the year 1898. I shall soon be returning to the arms of my dear wife, Mary, who has been patiently awaiting my return. I am happy to report that her former benefactress, Mrs. Cecil Forrester, has totally recovered her health, thanks in large part to the selfless ministrations of my wife.

I have only two matters of which to dispose. The widow Thoms has solved the one, by providing me with a sturdy metal box for these journals, as well as a secret compartment in the foundation wall of this home for their interment.

The second problem is of course the widow Thoms herself. The fire-damaged sanctuary at Grace Episcopal Church has now been restored, and the Thoms-Holmes nuptials have been re-scheduled for one week from today, on Saturday, October 22nd at 4 o'clock in the afternoon. However, Sherlock Holmes and one John H. Watson, M.D. have tickets for a train which will be departing Omaha's Union Station, destination New York City, at 9 o'clock tomorrow morning. Holmes and the widow Thoms are in the cellar this very moment, knocking a hole in the foundation wall. As I am writing this, I hear them coming up the stairs. You will forgive me if I pause for a moment to visit with them . . .

I can now report a happy ending to the widow Thoms business, at least as far as Sherlock Holmes is concerned. "Sherlock Holmes has convinced me," she just now said, "how important his work in England is. But he has promised when he retires, he will return to Omaha and marry me." She then ran into the other room to share this seemingly happy news with her young daughters.

"Have you lost your mind, Holmes?" I asked in astonishment. "Or has the widow begun to hallucinate?"

"Neither, dear chap," he replied with an uncharacteristic smile. "I have not lied to the lady, and I will hear no more talk on the subject."

"Of course," I agreed. "I shall never mention the widow Thoms again."

"Not at all," Holmes corrected. "Just never mention the subject of retiring."

THE END